RUNES
and
RAVENS

Familiar Spirits - Book 5

C H R I S T I N E   P O P E

RUNES AND RAVENS

Copyright © 2024 by Christine Pope

ISBN: 978-1-946435-77-4

Published by Dark Valentine Press

Cover design by Danielle Fine

Ebook formatting by Indie Author Services

Chapter 1

No Good Deed

"**T**hanks for shopping—have a great day," I said for what felt like about the fortieth time that afternoon.

Actually, I was almost positive it had to be at least the fortieth...or maybe the fiftieth. Salem, Massachusetts, was a hopping place the week leading up to Halloween, with tourists from all over the world descending to enjoy our particular brand of witchy thrills and chills. Most of the time, I just relaxed and rolled with it, since it was a lot of fun to watch how my hometown's visitors always seemed even more excited than usual by all the extra atmosphere, from the spooky displays in all the storefronts to the enormous pumpkin patch on Salem Common.

Now, though, I mostly wanted to hide in my house and not come out until it was all over.

"Are you okay, Charity?" my assistant Sage Halloran asked, and at once, I pulled a smile out of my pocket and slapped it on.

"Sure," I said. "I suppose the pace is starting to get to me. I'll be glad once Halloween is over and things settle down again."

She gave an understanding nod. At barely twenty-three, she was seven years younger than I and had only worked at my apothecary shop for a couple of years, so she hadn't quite had time to get jaded yet.

However, I knew world-weariness wasn't my real problem with the holiday. No, it was more that, no matter what I did, I couldn't seem to get past my breakup with Noah Jenkins a month earlier.

Everything had been going so well. I'd felt more connected to him than any other man I'd ever dated, even if I hadn't yet found the courage to tell him I was a witch. All the members of my coven— and probably the witchy community in Salem in general, which was large for a town of its size, thanks to our unique history—agreed that I'd been smart to take it slowly. We'd had centuries of hiding our true natures from the world, only divulging those secrets to a romantic partner once we were sure they were the person we wanted to be with for the rest of our lives. When you looked at the situation that way, it made sense that I hadn't said anything to Noah yet, since four months really wasn't that long when viewed in the grand scheme of things.

Unfortunately, he'd taken the exact opposite position on the situation. When he was kidnapped by Larissa Richter, a witch who dabbled in all kinds of dark magic, my coven and I had come to his rescue...and he'd found out I was a little bit more than simply a woman who owned an apothecary shop downtown and occasionally fostered animals on the side. Those animals were familiars, witch companions I worked with from time to time if tensions arose between them and their mistresses, thanks to my once-in-a-century gift of being able to talk to all familiars, no matter what shape they might take.

Anyway, since it had been glaringly obvious to Noah that I possessed all sorts of magical talents I hadn't bothered to divulge, he'd confronted me about my secrecy. I'd done my best to explain why I'd thought I had no choice but to keep silent about my magic until I was absolutely, positively sure about our relationship.

That conversation hadn't gone very well.

We hadn't spoken since then. Once or twice, I'd spied him in the local Market Basket, but he did his best to immediately push his shopping cart down another aisle and avoid me. And even though I desperately wanted another chance to talk to him and try to make him understand why I'd kept such an important matter a secret, I knew it wasn't a very good idea to force the issue in such a public place.

So that was where matters currently stood. I kept hoping the pain would go away at some point, but for now, I found myself moping a lot more than a grown woman of thirty probably should.

"It's kind of a lot," Sage agreed. She had light brown hair and hazel eyes, and her delicate features gave her a sort of elfin look. More than once, I thought she would have been a perfect candidate to dress up like a forest sprite at our local Renaissance Faire.

However, her tastes ran more to metal concerts when it came to the ways she occupied herself during her free time. It seemed she was always running down to Boston with friends to see one band or another, and was a lot more socially active than I'd been when I was fresh out of college. Back then, I'd done my best to keep a low profile and hadn't had a lot of mundane friends, just because it seemed safer that way. Sage, on the other hand, appeared to have successfully navigated the gulf between being a witch and still having a large social circle who knew absolutely nothing about the actual witches who lived in our town.

"But it pays the bills," I said with a smile, and she grinned back.

"That's for sure."

We didn't have time for any more conversation after that, because a huge group of older people entered the shop, on the hunt for my insomnia and arthritis elixirs and lord knows what else. The store often got deluged like that, thanks to the way tour buses loved to drop off their occupants at the stop only a few feet away from Full Moon Apothecary.

That was all right, though. When I was this busy, I didn't have as much time to think about how much I missed Noah Jenkins.

In a nod to the crowds that swarmed downtown Salem during the spooky season, I stayed open an extra half hour all through October. One year, I tried keeping the shop open to customers until six o'clock, but that wiped me out so much that I vowed never to do it again.

Even with closing everything down at five-thirty, I still didn't get home until close to six, since Sage and I had both decided it was better to stay a little late and tidy up rather than have to come in early to make sure the store was ready for that day's shoppers. And even though I only lived about ten minutes from Salem's downtown, my commute took more time than usual, thanks to the influx of tourists during that all-important week.

Despite the little ache in my soul that wouldn't go away, it still felt good to walk into my 1830s farmhouse, to be greeted by the familiar jumble of well-worn, mismatched furniture—and the two dogs I'd brought into my life. Milo was a cocker spaniel familiar whose mistress had been murdered back in late May, while Lexi was a dainty little long-haired chihuahua who had also lost an owner to murder. However, Lexi wasn't truly a familiar, but a regular dog who'd been granted the gift of speech by a powerful spell.

The two of them came running to the door as soon as I entered the house, and I bent so I could give them both pats on the head and some welcome back scratches. We'd all sort of agreed not to talk about Noah, as the dogs had both loved him, too, and probably missed him almost as much as I did.

"Was it busy?" Milo asked, and I nodded.

"Super busy," I replied. "And we still have almost a week until Halloween, so I have to believe it's only going to get crazier from here."

"But you're not going to work any later than you already are, right?" Lexi chimed in. Her pointy little face was full of concern, so I gave her an extra scratch behind the ears to reassure her.

"No, I'm not," I said. "People will just have to make it in during regular business hours. Just because it's Halloween doesn't mean I'm going to run myself ragged by staying open seven days a week."

Lexi's feathery tail wagged a little at that response, telling me she was glad to hear I hadn't changed my mind about working overtime. "Halloween is really important here, isn't it?"

"Very," I told her.

Her expression turned almost eager. "Does that mean you're going to get lots of trick-or-treaters here at our house?"

"Not really," I said, hating to crush her hopes. "It's really dark in this neighborhood, and the properties are far apart. Mostly, anyone with kids who lives around here takes them to the trick-or-treating we have downtown on Halloween."

At once, Lexi's sweet little face fell, so I knew I had to do what I could to reassure her.

"But that's okay," I went on, "because I'd already planned to bring you and Milo to the shop that day. Would you like to get dressed up?"

Her tail wagged at once, telling me she thought that was a great idea. She'd already informed me that her former owner, Milton Keyes, had dressed her in all kinds of sweaters and coats during the winter, so I'd started buying a few things for her... including the cutest little witch costume that I simply couldn't pass up when I'd spied it at PetSmart.

Milo, on the other hand, didn't seem nearly as

thrilled by the prospect of dressing up for Halloween. "I don't want to wear a costume," he declared, and I only smiled.

"And you don't have to," I assured him. "But maybe you'd be okay with wearing a bandana or something?"

That compromise seemed to work for him, because his tail wagged at once. "I could do that."

"Then it's settled," I said. "Now, let's see what we can scrounge for dinner."

Evening meals were definitely the worst. Then as now, Noah and I both had full-time jobs, so our opportunities for seeing each other in the middle of the day hadn't been exactly what you could call numerous. But while we were dating, we'd done our best to get together for dinner at least three or four times a week, often more, whether it was meeting at his place or coming over to my house.

Not so I could cook him a real meal—I was definitely not a kitchen witch—but we'd still gotten takeout, had spent dinner talking about our days...had gone upstairs to enjoy one another's company further after our relationship had progressed to that level.

And that was one thing I really, really didn't want to think about. My bed felt way too big without him in it, and even though I'd long since washed all the sheets and the blanket and quilt, I still fancied sometimes that I could smell the shampoo he used or his favorite sandalwood deodorant.

At least Lexi and Milo slept at the foot of the bed, so it wasn't as though I was utterly alone during the overnight hours. It could have been worse.

I supposed. The one good thing about the whole mess was that at least my mother hadn't pressured me to start dating again, as though she seemed to realize pushing me into seeing other men would only make matters worse.

All the same, I could tell that some people were starting to wonder exactly how long I planned to moon over Noah Jenkins. It wasn't as if we'd been seeing each other for years, or that we'd been engaged or anything close to it.

Hell, we hadn't even said "I love you."

Which was maybe part of the problem. I'd been waiting for him to say those words first, thinking that would be my signal to tell him about being a witch, about how I was different from most other women. And when we'd argued, I'd thrown that lack right in his face.

Obviously, he hadn't taken it very well.

Here we were, though. I'd made this lonely bed, so I'd have to lie in it.

The next day was Friday, and even busier than the Thursday that had preceded it. The crowds choking Salem would reach their crescendo seven days from now, on Halloween itself, but there were still plenty of people who seemed to think that being here the weekend before was good enough, especially if they couldn't take time off midweek.

Which was why I was less than thrilled to get a call late that afternoon from a number I'd never seen before. Usually, I tended to ignore my cell phone when things were busy at the store, but we had a quiet moment as one large group exited the shop, so I thought I might as well answer.

"This is Charity Hughes," I said.

A woman's voice, hesitant, almost wispy-sounding. "Oh, hello, Charity," she said. "My name is Sally Hawkins. I really need help with my familiar."

Hearing those words, I felt my stomach sink. Things had been quiet on the familiar-whisperer front for a while, and I would have much preferred to keep them that way. I had enough on my plate dealing with Halloween crowds and the apparently unending heartache that had followed Noah's exit from my life. The last thing I needed was to try to analyze a familiar's relationship with his witch mistress to discover what had gone wrong.

Unfortunately, I didn't have much choice in the matter. Years ago, after I'd realized what I could do with my talent, I'd sort of made it public in the witch community that I would always be available to help them with any issues they might be having with their familiars. Back then, I hadn't had anything close to resembling a personal life, so I hadn't thought nurturing familiars would be much of an imposition.

And all right, I didn't have much of a personal life right now, either, but I still didn't need anything else on an already full plate.

But I knew I couldn't turn Sally down, not when I could clearly hear the trembling edge of worry in her voice. I didn't think I knew her personally, but her name sounded sort of familiar, which made me think she must be from somewhere close.

My instincts were proved correct on that point, because she went on, "I'm just over in Middleton, so I could come by and see you after you've closed your shop for the day."

Clearly, she knew more about me than I did about her. "Sure," I said, although I knew my tone sounded way too guarded. "What kind of familiar do you have?"

"A raven," she replied. "His name is Edgar."

Of course it was. If I'd been feeling a little more snarky, I might have inquired as to whether her difficulty with her familiar had arisen from naming him after the man who wrote "The Raven."

But I didn't want to upset her any more than she already seemed to be. "And what's the problem with Edgar?"

A hesitation. "It's kind of complicated," Sally said. "I'd rather explain it to you in person."

That didn't sound very good. However, I could tell she didn't want me asking any more questions —and another group had just entered the shop, letting me know I needed to wrap up our conversation so I could get back to work.

"Okay," I said. "Come by at six. The address is 368 Winter Island Drive."

"Winter Island Drive," she repeated. "I'll be there—and thank you."

"It's no problem," I assured her.

After I ended the call, though, I found myself thinking it might turn out to be a very big problem after all.

Chapter 2

Nevermore

Sage seemed a little worried that I'd agreed to take on a client and her familiar with everything else that was going on...and I couldn't really blame her, since I was feeling pretty much the same way.

"Are you sure you're going to have time?" she asked as she locked the front door at a little past five-forty. The last couple of browsers had practically needed to be shooed from the shop, making me that much crankier. It wasn't as if I had unlimited time to loiter here, not with Sally Hawkins meeting me at my house in less than half an hour.

"I'll make the time," I said, knowing I sounded way too brusque. After all, Sage was only expressing a legitimate concern.

Her brow lifted, but it seemed she decided it wasn't a good idea to press me further on the subject. She came over to the cash register and deposited the front-door key in its designated compartment, then said, "What kind of familiar is it?"

"A raven," I replied.

Now both her brows went up. "Have you ever worked with a raven before?"

"No," I said. "A budgie once, but that's not really the same thing."

Sage grinned. "That's for sure. But ravens are super-smart, so it might not be too hard to get to the bottom of what's going on."

I could only hope so. When you got down to it, though, pretty much all familiars were much smarter than the average specimens of their species —they had to be, since they provided emotional support for their witches and sometimes helped with spell-casting or any other small chores that might take a part of the burden off their magical mistresses.

So did that mean Sally Hawkins' raven familiar would be scary-smart?

I supposed I'd find out soon enough.

Traffic was even worse that night than it had been the day before, which meant I got to my house about five minutes later than I'd hoped. A white

Subaru Forester was parked off to one side of the driveway, telling me that Sally had beaten me there.

Holding back a sigh, I made myself climb out of my ancient Land Rover Discovery—a vehicle I'd purchased because I figured it would help me with hauling around whatever familiars I might be babysitting at any particular time—and go over to meet Sally, who'd also just emerged from her car. She was small and slight, a few inches shorter than I and even more slender, with mousy hair that just reached her shoulders. I couldn't really guess her age, but if pressed, I probably would have said she was about fifteen years older than I, maybe a little more.

A large raven, one who was a little larger than Lexi from beak to tail, was perched on the woman's forearm, making her look even more fragile. She gave me a grateful smile as I approached and said, "Hi, Charity. I'm Sally Hawkins."

Probably an unnecessary introduction, since who else could she be? However, I only said, "Hi, Sally. Sorry I'm late—traffic was crazy."

"Yes, I ran into some of it myself," she responded as she followed me up the walk to the front door. My street didn't have any official illumi-nation, but I'd set small lights along the stone path that everyone in the neighborhood thought were solar but in fact were powered by a very low-level enchantment. "It feels like the whole world comes to Salem at Halloween."

"It does," I agreed. Just as I was about to turn the knob, I added, "I have two dogs, Milo and Lexi. Milo is a familiar, and Lexi is a regular dog with a spell placed on her that allows her to talk to witches. Will Edgar have a problem with them?"

Before Sally could reply, the raven stretched his wings, not quite flapping them, but letting me know he'd heard my question and wanted to reply for himself.

"No, he's fine with all other animals," Sally said. "That is, I don't have any pets, but he seems more interested in the rabbits and squirrels that come into my yard than anything else."

Well, that was good to hear. Even Lexi, at a whopping eight pounds, was probably too big for Edgar to regard her as prey, but better to make sure before I allowed Sally and her familiar to enter the house.

There had been no way for me to call home and let Milo and Lexi know I'd be having company, so as Sally and I stepped into the living room, I called out, "Lexi! Milo! We have visitors!"

The two dogs came bounding into the room and then stopped suddenly, a little taken aback despite my warning. Milo glanced over at me.

"Edgar is a familiar," I said. "And this is Sally,

his mistress. She and I are going to have a little chat."

"What about dinner?" Lexi asked. Sally looked a little startled despite my comment earlier about my dog's ability to communicate; I supposed it had to be disconcerting to hear an animal speak who wasn't your familiar.

"I'll get you some kibble," I replied.

"Oh, yes," Sally broke in, clearly trying to do her best to help. "You do what you need to. Edgar and I will wait in here."

I decided it would probably be better not to say that the dogs weren't nearly as concerned about getting their kibble as they were about how long my conversation with Sally might delay their real dinner, the one where they begged all kinds of scraps off my plate. No, instead I went into the kitchen, dutifully filled their bowls, and then said in a low voice, "I don't know how long this is going to take, and it's obvious Sally is worried about her familiar, so please don't come in and bother us while we're trying to talk."

"We would not," Milo said, big brown eyes indignant. "We know your work with familiars is important."

Lexi's tail made a half-hearted wag. "Even though it seems like you're really too busy right now to take on another responsibility."

I wouldn't permit myself to roll my eyes, not

when I knew they were only worried about me. "It'll be fine," I said. "Honestly, I don't even know what the problem is. Maybe it's something that can be cleared up with a quick chat."

Both dogs looked dubious, and I couldn't say I blamed them. Nothing in my life had gone too smoothly lately.

But they didn't say anything else, and I hurried back out to the living room, where Sally had sat down on the well-worn leather couch, Edgar still perched on her arm. He looked awfully heavy, so I said, "Edgar can sit on the sofa, too, if you want to give your arm a break."

At once, he fluttered away from her and settled himself on the opposite arm of the couch. She lowered the limb, expression grateful.

"Thank you," she said simply.

"Can I get you anything?" I asked, realizing I hadn't been the best hostess. "Water, tea?"

"No, I'm fine," Sally replied. "I don't want to impose any more than I already have. I just didn't know who else to turn to."

Something I'd heard many times before from witches having trouble with their familiars. After all, it wasn't the sort of thing a regular vet could help you with.

But I didn't want to think about veterinarians, because that would only lead my thoughts back to

Noah Jenkins, and I had enough to worry about right now.

"It's fine," I assured her as I settled myself in the flowered armchair opposite the couch. My mother had been about to donate the chair years earlier, and I'd snagged it for my own despite her protestations that it had done its service for our family and needed to move on.

No way, though. The fabric might have been worn in places, but it was still the comfiest chair I'd ever sat in.

The clock ticking on the mantel told me I might as well get on with things. "So...what's going on with Edgar?"

Sally pressed her lips together. She wasn't wearing a wedding ring—not that strange, since many witches opted for a solitary life—and she reached inside the brown purse she had looped over one arm so she could pull out a small velvet pouch, the sort of thing you might use to store a deck of Tarot cards or maybe a few tumbled crystals.

In this case, though, the bag didn't contain cards or crystals, but instead a set of smooth, polished stones engraved with angular figures.

Rune stones.

I never used runes—heck, I hardly used the Tarot—but I knew a lot of witches utilized them for divination and general advice from the universe.

"You want to tell my fortune?" I asked, holding back a smile.

Sally Hawkins, on the other hand, didn't look amused at all. "No, that's not what they're for."

Even as she spoke, Edgar hopped off the arm of the couch where he'd been perched and landed on the coffee table. Leaning forward, he used his long, heavy beak to separate several rune stones from the rest of the group and then turned so I was fixed by his bright brown eye.

"That's what he's been doing for the past week," Sally said. "He won't talk to me at all. He just uses those stones to communicate."

It wasn't the first time I'd dealt with a familiar who'd suddenly stopped speaking for some reason —that was why Darla Fitzgerald, Milo's former mistress, had come to me back in May—but the whole setup with the runes was a new one.

"So...what did he just tell us?"

Now Sally looked almost abashed. "I'm not sure," she said. "I mean, each of the runes has its own meaning, but even those meanings are open for interpretation, depending on who's doing the reading. So this one"—she touched a fingertip to a stone whose carving looked like a capital "I"— "means Ice, but it's not like it's predicting the weather or something. It's more a sensation of being stuck, like being caught in the ice."

"Sort of like the Hanged Man in Tarot," I murmured, still staring down at the stones, and Sally nodded.

"Right. But why did Edgar pull that one, along with the Yew and the one that means 'Journey'?" She shook her head, and her raven ruffled his feathers, giving every indication that he was supremely annoyed by her cluelessness.

Well, the problem was, Edgar knew what he was trying to communicate, but his mistress was still in the dark, and I certainly had no idea what he was trying to say, either. If I'd known anything about runes, I might have been in a different position, but....

I told myself I'd worry about teaching myself a new divination skill later. Right now, it seemed more important to try to get the timeline that would clarify when Sally's familiar had decided to clam up and use the stones to communicate instead of speaking to her normally.

"You said he started doing this about a week ago?" I asked, and she nodded. "Did anything unusual happen around then, anything that stood out?"

"Nothing at all," she replied at once. "I might be a witch, but I don't have what you could call an interesting life—I work from home as a call center manager."

I was forced to admit that it certainly didn't sound like a thrilling existence. Like many witches, Sally had gravitated toward a vocation that would allow her to work from home—just like my mother, although I had to admit that my mom's current career as a cottage-core influencer on Instagram was a little more interesting, even if I still couldn't say for sure exactly what she did.

"So, one day Edgar just up and decided to start talking to you with runes?"

Sally spread her hands, looking helpless. "Basically. Believe me, I've been wracking my brains, trying to remember if anything had happened that might have set him off, and I can't think of a single thing."

None of this sounded very promising, but I told myself I needed to keep pushing on. "Is he with you all day?"

"Mostly," she said. "That is, he goes out in the morning to take a flight around the neighborhood and then again in the evening, but otherwise he's either in the house or pecking around in the yard. I made sure to buy a house that sat on a big piece of land so he'd have plenty of space to keep himself amused."

Some people might have wondered how a woman with a fairly modest work-from-home job would be able to afford a property like that, but I knew we witches often had generational wealth to work with...and also weren't above utilizing small prosperity spells from time to time to provide even more of a cushion. Not the sort of thing that would be noticed by the general public, but enough to keep us comfortable.

"And there was no sign that he might have encountered another witch who decided to cast a spell on him, for whatever reason?"

Now Sally looked almost indignant. "Of course not," she said. "Our coven in Middleton is small and friendly. There are only five of us witches in the whole town, and I've known all of them my entire life. I know no one would have any reason to cast a spell like that on Edgar." She paused there, as if deciding whether she should say anything else, then went on, "Honestly, none of us are all that powerful. I'm not sure whether anyone in my coven would even be able to cast a spell like that."

Probably not the sort of thing she was thrilled to admit to me, but at least I got the feeling she was being honest. Just like regular people, witches varied greatly in their abilities and fields of specialty, so I didn't see anything strange in what Sally had just confessed about her coven. We witches in Salem tended to be stronger than average, mostly because our powers were the result of generations of magic concentrating in one place, but that didn't mean every town's coven was like mine.

So all right, maybe no one that Sally knew directly had been responsible for Edgar's shift in behavior. That didn't mean another witch might not have cast the spell on him, although I had no idea why anyone would want to do something like that, except maybe as a mean-spirited prank.

The raven let out a harsh croak of a noise, then leaned down again and pushed another stone toward me. The runes were made of polished tiger-eye with engraved gold markings, very handsome.

This one looked almost like an "H," although one with the crosspiece drawn at a slight angle rather than directly across. I sent a questioning look at Sally.

"I think that one's called 'Hagalaz.' It means things that are out of our control...or at least, that's the meaning I found online."

Was Edgar trying to tell us that what had happened to him was something that had nothing to do with Sally...or with witches in general?

I might have been reaching with that one. It was probably much more likely that his current mode of communication wasn't anything he'd chosen on purpose.

Which led us right back to who might have done this to him.

What I didn't know about runes would have

filled several books on its own, but I knew enough to realize that speaking through them had to be very difficult. Even a pendulum or a Ouija board at least gave you simple yes/no answers, whereas the runes tended to be much more open to interpretation.

My usual go-to for situations where I felt out of my depth on witchy lore was Grace Bowersby, a member of my coven and a sort of unofficial witch historian. However, I'd known Grace all my life, and I couldn't recall her ever working with runes. Like a lot of us, she tended to use the Tarot if she needed some form of outside guidance.

That didn't mean I wouldn't do my best to pick her brain as soon as I could.

Probably not right away, though. I was already tired and hadn't even eaten dinner yet, and I didn't want to intrude on her tonight. While the situation with Edgar was perplexing, nothing about it screamed emergency, especially since I often kept familiars for several days while I tried to get to the bottom of whatever issue they were having with their mistresses.

"Have you had any interactions with any witches outside your coven?" I asked next. Sally Hawkins didn't seem like the sort of person who would ruffle many feathers...so to speak...but I couldn't rule out a grudge from someone who didn't live in Middleton, someone whom Sally might have offended.

She shook her head, though. "I live a quiet life, Charity. I work from home, and I meet with my coven for our book club twice a month." A small smile touched her lips as she added, "That's what we call our meetings, just so no one thinks it's strange that we get together as often as we do."

An interesting ruse. "And you've never had a mundane try to join?"

Her smile widened. "Oh, once or twice. But if that happens, we choose the most boring book we can think of as the one we're supposed to be discussing that week, and that gets rid of the eager beavers."

I supposed it would. The mental scenario made me smile a little, too, even while I knew we needed to be focused on the situation with Edgar.

If Sally was to be believed, though—and I didn't see any reason why she shouldn't be—it sure seemed as if she was leading a pretty unremarkable life, and wasn't the kind of person who should have attracted a dark spell, especially one that had struck at her familiar. I'd encountered that kind of skullduggery before, but I still thought it was one of the most underhanded things a witch could do. If you had a beef with someone, you should take it directly to them and not involve an innocent animal.

I glanced over at Edgar, whose dark eyes met mine, oddly frank, almost as though he expected me to get to the bottom of this without any problem.

Or maybe he was just wondering why we humans were so dense, in which case, I could sort of agree with him. Right then, I was feeling pretty flummoxed.

"Well," I said, "it seems like you should probably leave him with me for a few days, if that's all right. Generally, my methods work best when I have enough time with a familiar to get to know them and allow them to get comfortable with me."

Sally's lips pursed, and her gaze strayed to her familiar before returning to me. "I know that's how you like to do things," she replied. "But having a raven around isn't the same thing as having a dog."

At the all-important "D" word, both Milo's and Lexi's ears perked up. They'd stayed quiet during the entire conversation, clearly understanding that this wasn't a matter they should get involved in, but I could tell they'd been following along.

"Oh, I know," I said. "I've watched birds before, although not any as big as Edgar. But I've also had a hedgehog, a raccoon, a fox, and even a pygmy goat one time. It's not like I'm not used to having unusual animals around."

Those words seemed to reassure Sally, because

she shifted toward the back of the couch, even if she didn't completely lean against it. "He eats an unusual diet," she told me. "Mealworm cakes and a mix of ground beef and pellets, depending on what he's in the mood for."

I could deal with the ground beef. Even mealworm cakes weren't the end of the world, although I'd have to run to the pet store in the morning if Sally hadn't brought any along with her.

"It's fine," I responded, hoping I sounded completely unconcerned about Edgar's mealtime preferences. "Did you bring some of his food with you?"

She nodded. "I thought I'd better, just in case. There's a pack in my trunk with his things."

"Then you might as well fetch it," I said. "This is something that's going to take me some time to figure out. Not too much, I hope," I added hastily as alarm flared in Sally's eyes. "But I want to make sure Edgar has all his things here so he's comfortable."

"I understand. Let me go out to my car."

She got up from the sofa and headed toward the door, leaving me alone with the raven. He gazed back at me for a moment, then bent his neck again to push a single stone toward me, one that looked like a sort of flag, with two wavy lines protruding from a single vertical line.

I had no idea what it meant...but I had a feeling I'd find out soon.

Chapter 3

Rune My Day

The rune stone Edgar had pushed toward me the night before stood for communication, which I supposed made some sense. After all, Sally Hawkins had left him with me precisely so we could start some kind of dialogue.

My worries about having a raven in the house had mostly abated after an uneventful night. His mistress had left food for him, along with a tattered blanket she said was his and a collection of shiny objects that included a small chunk of pyrite, a cubic zirconia ring with one of its stones missing, a bottle cap, and a piece of sea glass. According to Sally, he had a larger collection at home, but these were the items he absolutely needed to have with him at all times.

Which was fine. My house had its own brand

of clutter, so adding a few more pieces wasn't going to make much of a difference.

And even though Milo and Lexi couldn't speak to him directly the way they might have with a familiar who wasn't suffering his particular affliction, they were both very kind, leading him out back to see the yard. He immediately flapped his wings and took to the air, and for a worried moment or two, I wondered if I would have to hop on my broomstick to keep track of him.

To my infinite relief, though, he only circled in the air above the house before landing in the yard so he could pick around in the grass and look for interesting insects. The two dogs kept him company while doing their best to stay out of his way, and all in all, I could tell they would take good care of him while I was at work.

Since it seemed to me he could understand everything I was saying even though he couldn't answer in words, I addressed him directly before I headed out that morning.

"I have to go to work at my shop," I said. "But I'll come home at lunch to check on you and see how you're doing."

His wings gave a small flap in response, which I hoped meant he knew what I was telling him and that it wouldn't be a problem.

Most of the time, I wouldn't have bothered coming home for my midday meal, especially when the shop was as busy as I knew it was going to be today, the Saturday before Halloween. Staying away for almost eight hours didn't seem like a very good idea, though, so I'd come up with this compromise. At least it would only take me twenty minutes round trip, which meant I wouldn't need a whole hour away.

After admonishing all the animals to be good in my absence, I headed outside so I could walk over to the detached garage and get in my SUV. It was a beautiful day, the sky a deep sapphire with some puffy white clouds floating by, the wind from the ocean brisk and heavily scented with salt. Cold, though, enough that I was glad I'd remembered to button my coat before I left the house.

Not for the first time, I found myself wishing the property had an attached garage, but that just wasn't something you got with a vintage farm-house—at least, not one that hadn't been remodeled within an inch of its life. I'd done a few upgrades after I bought the place a couple of years earlier, mostly because the former owners hadn't touched anything since the 1990s and the kitchen and bathrooms were in desperate need of a makeover, but the only way to have the garage attached would have been to demo the whole thing and build it in the spot my herb garden currently occupied. There was no way in the world I would do anything so destructive to my yard, which meant I had to resign myself to trudging through the snow in the winter and rainstorms in the spring and summer.

Traffic was heavy, as I'd expected, but I'd left the house early enough that I still got to the store about a quarter before the hour. Because Sage and I had tidied up the evening before, there wasn't much for me to do besides stock the cash register and get out the key for the front door...although there was no way I'd unlock the shop before ten. Seven and a half hours of dealing with customers was quite enough for me.

Several people already waited on the sidewalk outside, and I did my best to pay no attention to the way they kept staring in the front window or ostentatiously examined the store hours posted on the door. After a lifetime of dealing with my mother, I'd gotten pretty good at ignoring things when there wasn't any other acceptable alternative.

Sage arrived just a few minutes before ten, looking harried, which was definitely not the norm for her. "Sorry I'm late," she said, sounding breathless. "But someone took my space out back, and I had to park three blocks away."

I frowned. The store had two parking spaces allotted to it, with clear signage that they were for employees only. However, when the hordes descended, rules like that tended to get thrown out the window.

"Do you want me to call parking enforcement?" I asked. "We can have them towed."

Sage shook her head. "No, it's okay. I don't want to piss off someone who could be a potential customer."

I supposed she had a point there, but the situation was still annoying. There wasn't time to argue about it, though, because the clock on the wall told me it was now a minute until ten, and that meant we needed to open the front door right on the hour.

"Okay," I said. "Then I suppose it's time to get this party started."

At several points that morning, I honestly wondered whether I would be able to break away and run home for lunch after all, but the steady flow of customers began to ease just a little after twelve, letting me know the tourists were more interested in eating than shopping right then.

"I'll be as fast as I can," I told Sage, and she only lifted her shoulders.

"It's fine," she said. "I mean, we're all entitled to a lunch break. If I get a rush, people are just going to have to suck it up and wait their turn."

A practical way of looking at the situation. All the same, I thanked her as I hurried out, and said again that I wouldn't take any more time than I absolutely had to.

As I pulled out of my parking space, I wondered whether it would even be there when I got back. Unlike Sage, I wasn't too thrilled by the prospect of having to walk blocks to get to the store, especially on a day when I probably wouldn't have a single chance to sit down.

But since it couldn't be helped, I just backed out the Discovery and uttered a small charm under my breath, one that would make my parking space supremely unattractive to anyone who might pass by during my absence.

Most of the traffic seemed to be concentrated downtown, so I made better time than I'd expected. When I pulled into the driveway—I wasn't going to waste time putting my SUV in the garage—everything looked just the way I'd left it, the white-painted house serene in the coolly bright October sun, the mums and asters in the front flowerbeds blooming bravely, even though their days were now numbered.

And as I came into the living room, it was to find the two dogs sleeping in front of the hearth, while Edgar was perched on one of the arms of the sofa, head drooping a little. His blanket was pulled up on the cushion nearest him, and his piece of pyrite glinted in the sun that slanted in the windows.

Once I shut the door, though, all three animals woke up at once, with Milo and Lexi running over so they could sniff my jean-clad legs—even though they knew exactly what I smelled like when I came home from my shop—and Edgar roused himself so he could gaze at me with a pair of bright brown eyes.

"How'd it go?" I asked, although I could already tell that everything had been peaceful at the house.

"Fine," Milo told me. "We just stayed in here and slept, mostly. A couple of times, Edgar looked out the window. Lexi and I tried to show him how to use the dog door, but he didn't seem interested."

I could imagine. While ravens seemed to be perfectly fine with waddling around on the ground while looking for bugs—or maybe shiny things for their collections—I didn't know if those ground-based activities were enough to make them all right with going in and out of a doggy door. Mine was a nice one with clear plastic flaps and magnets to hold the flaps in place once the dogs had gone through it, but I could see how it might be kind of intimidating to a bird who'd never seen anything like that before.

"Well, maybe he'll get used to it after another day or so," I said. "But I'm glad you all had a quiet time. How about some lunch?"

That question got the dogs' tails wagging, and

even Edgar spread his wings and flapped them. Inside my cluttered living room, their span seemed impressively large, and I hoped he wouldn't knock over the table lamp located only a few feet away.

Luckily, there weren't any mishaps, and the trio followed me into the kitchen. Soon enough, I'd dispensed dry dog food for Lexi and Milo, and an unappetizing mix of raw ground beef and meal-worms for Edgar, and all three of them were munching away happily.

Fixing the raven's food hadn't done great things for my appetite, but I made myself a ham and cheese sandwich anyway, knowing I needed to eat so I'd have the stamina to get through the rest of the afternoon at work. The animals finished their meals first, of course, and I set down my partially eaten sandwich so I could let them outside to get some fresh air, a little ritual of ours even though they could have used the dog door. Edgar had already proven to me that he had no plans to escape and would only circle above the house a few times before coming back to land, which meant I could finish my meal without having to continu-ally check to make sure everything was okay out there.

All the same, I took my phone with me to the back patio, where I sat down on one of the chairs— I really needed to remember to store the cushions in the garage, since we were well past outdoor living at that point in the season—and called Grace Bowersby.

She sounded a little surprised to hear from me, which I'd expected. Although the coven got together at the new and the full moons and the major witchy holidays...Yule, Imbolc, Beltane... everything had been pretty quiet for the past month, and I'd had no reason to reach out to my coven members beyond the agreed-upon meeting times.

"I have a new client," I told Grace, then launched into a short explanation of why Sally Hawkins had brought Edgar to me. I finished by saying, "I don't have much experience with runes, which was why I thought I should pick your brain."

A short silence, and then Grace said, "I'm afraid I don't have a lot of experience with them, either. As far as I know, no one in our coven does. We prefer to work with the Tarot if we need any outside guidance."

Something I'd already known, and I barely held back a sigh. "So, there isn't anything you can tell me?"

Now she chuckled. "Well, there's always something. And you know how I love having something new to research. Why don't you let me dig up what I can this afternoon, and then you can swing by and we can talk about what I've found?"

That sounded like a great idea. As far as I could tell, Edgar hadn't even reached for the runes this morning, as if he'd known I would be of even less use working with them than his mistress had been. But if Grace could do some of the heavy lifting for me while I was at work for the rest of the day, then I might be a little better equipped to try communicating with the raven afterward.

"Perfect," I said. "Is around five forty-five okay with you? I've been staying open a little late this week and the next to handle all the Halloween shoppers."

"It's fine," Grace replied immediately, which was pretty much what I'd expected. She was retired and didn't have a lot to fill her days, except for the times when she'd hop over to Seabrook to see her granddaughter. Grandchild number two was expected any day, though, which meant my unlimited claims on Grace's time might come to an end very soon.

In the meantime, I'd be happy to hear whatever she was able to discover.

I thanked her and said I'd see her late this afternoon, then ended the call. By that point, Edgar had landed on the grass and joined Milo and Lexi out in the sun, and I beckoned them all to come inside. Under other circumstances, I would have let them stay out there a while longer so they could enjoy the friendly weather, but I didn't have that luxury today.

No, I needed to head back to the store.

I let them know I had to make a fast stop on the way home from work but that I shouldn't be any later than six-thirty, then headed to the driveway so I could climb in the Discovery and drive back downtown. Traffic was even more of a snarl than it had been when I left, but, to my infinite relief, it seemed my charm had worked, since no one had taken my parking space.

It was the little things that helped.

There was a line at the cash register when I made my way to the front of the store, so I took over from Sage, telling her she needed to get out of there and grab something to eat. Looking relieved, she bobbed her head and made her escape, probably to the sandwich store down the block since she didn't need to worry about going home.

And after that, I didn't have much time to think about anything. The customers kept coming, and I'd already sold out of a few popular items. That meant I'd need to spend my days off on Sunday and Monday making more rather than relaxing, but I told myself it was okay. At least this way, I'd keep myself busy and wouldn't have any time to spare to brood about the Noah Jenkins–sized hole in my life.

Sage and I took turns at the cash register all

afternoon, giving the other person a chance to wander the store and answer any questions—and, in one case, to prevent a couple of teenage girls from helping themselves to a five-finger discount from my incense display.

They giggled and tried to act as if it wasn't that big a deal. Someone made of sterner stuff might have called the police, but I didn't want to get them into any permanent trouble. Instead, I told them that stealing was bad karma and that I definitely would contact the authorities if I caught them doing anything like that again, eliciting another round of careless giggles before they left, apparently heading to the candle shop next door.

Well, at least it would probably be harder to steal a jar candle than it would a few sticks of incense.

By the time five-thirty rolled around, I was definitely over it and just wanted to go home. I knew that wasn't an option, though, not when I needed to stop at Grace Bowersby's house first. With any luck, the visit wouldn't take very long, and I'd be able to finally get back to my house and put my feet up and have a glass of wine.

Or two.

"Can you take out the trash?" I asked Sage. "I need to put all this money and these receipts in the safe."

It wasn't like the store was Fort Knox or

anything close to it. However, I had a small safe that I kept in the break area in the storeroom for those days—like this one—when I closed up after the banks had closed as well, and any deposits would need to be made the following morning on the way into work.

"Sure," Sage said, and grabbed the plastic garbage bag that had been getting steadily more packed full of flotsam and jetsam as the day wore on. In general, we didn't generate a lot of trash unless I'd gotten a shipment of apothecary jars or something and had a lot of packing material to dispose of. However, we'd been busy enough that people had left behind drinks and food wrappers when they thought we weren't looking, and there wasn't much we could do about the mess except grumble a few choice words about slobs under our breaths and then throw the abandoned cups and other rubbish into the trash.

She grabbed the bag and headed out back, where we shared a dumpster with the other occupants of this row of businesses. However, she'd barely been gone for a minute before she came back.

"Um, Charity?" she said, voice uncharacteristically hesitant, and I turned away from the cash register, pouch of money still in one hand.

Her face was dead pale. Yes, she was light-skinned, if not as fair as I was, with my redhead's complexion, but still, I'd never seen her appear that way before, and I found myself tensing, as if in anticipation of the shock I somehow knew was coming.

"What's the matter?" I asked, taking a step toward her. Honestly, she looked as though she was about to pass out.

Sage swallowed.

"I just found a dead body behind the dumpster."

Chapter 4

Throwaway Notions

S age and I sat in my makeshift break area—
really, just a screened-off section of the
stock room—while Derek Falco took
notes.

If the situation hadn't been so serious, I might
have reflected on the irony of Derek being the one
to come out to my store and lead the investigation.
True, Salem only had two detectives who worked
homicide, so the odds were pretty much fifty-fifty
that he'd be the one to show up, but still.

"Did either of you notice anything unusual
today?" he asked.

Sage and I glanced at each other, and I saw the
way her mouth twisted a little.

"You mean, unusual besides finding a dead
woman by the dumpster?" she responded.

He didn't smile. It had been more than a month since I'd seen him in person, and I was struck again by how good-looking he was, with that jet-black hair and equally dark eyes, those sculpted features that looked as though they could have belonged to a statue standing in the courtyard of a Venetian palazzo.

I still thought Noah was the handsomer of the two, but I also couldn't deny that Derek Falco was a damn gorgeous specimen of a man.

"Yes, besides that," Derek said.

"It was a busy day," I told him after noting the way Sage had hesitated. Normally, she wasn't what I would call a reserved person, but the grisly discovery of a few minutes ago had clearly shaken her to the core.

As for myself, well, this wasn't the first time death had crossed my path during the past few months, so I supposed I looked more outwardly composed than my assistant did. Inwardly...well, I'd already started to wonder and worry about who could have done such a thing.

And whether they planned to strike again.

"Lots of customers," I went on. "Honestly, neither of us was able to leave the shop at all except to get something to eat."

"Where did you go?" he asked me, and something about the way his gaze caught mine made me wonder if there was some kind of subtext to the question beyond getting an accounting of my movements.

"Home," I said shortly. "I needed to check on my animals. I had a sandwich and came back about twenty minutes later."

He made a few notes on the yellow pad he held, then looked over at Sage. "Did you go out for lunch?"

"Yes," she replied. "I went down the street to Henry's and ate there. I was probably gone about twenty minutes, tops."

"And did you notice anyone unusual loitering around the shop or anywhere else in the vicinity?"

Sage sent him a look that still managed to have something of withering scorn in it, despite the recent shock she'd suffered. "Um, it's less than a week until Halloween. This town is full of 'unusual' people."

Definitely not an understatement. The holiday itself might have still been days away, but that hadn't deterred a lot of our visitors from dressing up in their versions of "witchy" garb—flowing black skirts, pointy black hats, goth-looking jackets and boots—or even actual Halloween costumes, everything from vampires to zombies and other creatures of the night. With so many bedecked tourists crowding the sidewalks, the people dressed in regular street clothes were the ones who actually stood out.

Now Derek's mouth finally quirked, although his voice sounded sober enough as he said, "Duly noted. Did any of your customers stand out to you in any way?"

I thought of the two girls I'd caught trying to shoplift incense. Yes, one could say they "stood out," but I highly doubted either of them was capable of murder.

"Not that I can think of," I replied, and Sage nodded.

"It was super busy, and I had a couple of Karens to deal with, but not anyone who seemed like a murderer."

Again, Derek's mouth lifted at the corners. At least he seemed clued in enough to realize that the "Karen" epithet only meant an entitled, annoying customer and not someone actually named that, because he didn't ask for further clarification. Instead, he inquired, "Did you notice anything strange when you went to the dumpster?"

"Just a dead body."

His gaze flickered to me for a moment, and I saw at once the way his eyes glinted with amusement. "I meant, was there any sign of a struggle, anything that the killer might have disturbed while they were back there?"

Now Sage's expression grew serious, and her fawn-brown eyebrows pulled together as she appeared to reconstruct the scene in her mind.

"Not that I can think of," she replied after a moment. "It was quiet—the stores on either side of us closed at the regular time, so everyone who works there had already gone home. The light on the rear wall of the candle shop was on, so I could see everything pretty clearly. That's why I was able to see the dead woman's feet sticking out from behind the dumpster." Sage paused there, then pressed her lips together. "One of her shoes was missing. It was kind of awful."

"Did you find it?" I asked abruptly, and Derek turned his gaze toward me.

"Find what?"

"The missing shoe," I said, and his eyes narrowed for a moment.

"Not so far," he replied, still frowning slightly. "Do you think that's important somehow?"

I couldn't say for sure. Or rather, I couldn't say what I'd really been thinking, that sometimes practitioners of dark magic would remove items of interest from a victim to aid them in their enchantments. To know for sure, however, I'd need to talk to Elise Figg, the only member of my coven who ever worked with those sorts of spells.

"Probably not," I said, hoping that my hesitation hadn't been too obvious. "It just seems like a strange detail."

Now he shrugged, saying, "Not necessarily. It'll take some time to determine whether the victim was killed here or was murdered somewhere else and then dropped off behind the shop. It's possible the murderer had intended to put the victim inside the dumpster and then abandoned the scene when Sage came out to dump the trash."

My assistant didn't look overly convinced by that theory. "Wouldn't I have heard someone running away if they'd been back there the whole time?"

"Maybe," Derek allowed. "Or maybe not. It's not as if you would have been listening for someone, would you?"

Judging by the way her shoulders lifted a fraction, it seemed he'd made a point there. "No, I guess I wasn't. I was just hurrying because it had been a long day and I wanted to go home."

A sentiment I shared equally. Too bad our day had been made even longer by Sage's grisly discovery and the ensuing investigation. I knew that while Derek was talking to the two of us, his deputies were out back combing the crime scene for any shred of evidence they could find.

And although I understood that this question-and-answer session with Derek was a necessary part of the process, I really didn't know what he thought we had to offer to clarify the situation. However, I tried to remind myself that in my own murder investigations, it had often been the weird little snippets of details that broke the case for me, so I couldn't fault him for being thorough, even while I wanted nothing more than to get out of there and go back to my house so I could surround myself with its familiar comforts and do my best to hope this was a random act of violence and nothing more.

To my relief, he closed his notebook and tucked it into the interior breast pocket of his jacket, seeming to signal that he'd gotten enough from us for now.

"Thank you for your cooperation," he said, now sounding more formal. "If any other questions come up during the course of the investigation, I'll be in touch."

Sage, looking just as relieved as I felt, got up from her chair. "So, I can go?"

"Yes," Derek replied. "Enjoy the rest of your Saturday night."

She bolted out of the break room like she'd been shot out of a cannon, telling me she had plans and was already running late for them. I, on the other hand, didn't have anything on the schedule besides dropping by Grace Bowersby's house, although I'd need to text her to make sure it was still okay for me to come by even though I'd be almost a half hour late.

Derek looked over at me. "What about you?"

"What about me?" I said, realizing even as the

words left my mouth how stupid they must have sounded.

A faint smile pulled at his lips. "Do you have plans tonight?"

Oh, boy. There was no reason in the world for Derek Falco to know that I'd broken up with Noah Jenkins a month earlier...except for the part where he was a detective and talked to people all day long, and had probably picked something up from the grapevine.

It sure felt as though he'd thought enough time had elapsed that it was okay to make a move.

Or I could have been interpreting the situation completely wrong.

Either way, I had a ready excuse. Maybe some people would have thought I was crazy for pushing Derek away, but my heart wasn't over Noah.

I didn't know whether it would ever be.

Also, there was the much more practical aspect to the situation, which was that we witches tended to steer clear of law enforcement whenever we could, thanks to the way we had to keep our magic hidden. Getting involved with a detective on the Salem P.D. didn't seem like a very good idea.

"I was supposed to go over to a friend's house after work," I said, my tone steady. "In fact, I need to text her to make sure it's still okay even though I'm running late."

Something about his posture seemed to relax

slightly, as if he was glad to hear that my "friend" was female and therefore not a possible romantic rival.

Or again, I could have been reading way too much into his reaction.

"Then I won't keep you," he said.

I smiled. "Oh, you're not keeping me." I realized then that during his discussion with Sage and me, he'd never mentioned the victim's name. Maybe he didn't know; I supposed it was possible she hadn't carried any identification. Still, I figured it couldn't hurt to ask. "Who was she? The victim, I mean."

The faint smile he'd been wearing vanished. "Her name was Eunice Bartlett. Sixty-two years old. Her I.D. had a Boston address, so my people are following up on that and trying to locate her next of kin."

Why in the world would someone want to bludgeon a sixty-two-year-old woman to death? I supposed robbery could have been the motive, but if that was the case, then you'd think her purse—and therefore her driver's license—would have been missing.

"That's terrible," I said, and Derek nodded.

"It is. But we'll get to the bottom of it. You have a good evening."

He headed out then, and I retrieved my phone from my purse so I could text Grace.

"This is just terrible," she said after I'd sat down in her chintz-decorated living room and accepted a glass of water. "You say Sage found the victim behind a dumpster?"

"Yes," I replied, then helped myself to a welcome swallow of water. That talk with Derek had made me thirsty. "An older woman named Eunice Bartlett. It sounds like she's from Boston."

Hearing that piece of information, Grace stared at me in shock. She was also in her early sixties, with curly fair hair she usually kept pulled back in a low bun at the back of her neck and a plump, cheerful face. "Eunice Bartlett?" she repeated.

I gazed back at her, equally startled. "You knew her?"

"Well, not exactly," Grace said. "That is, she was fairly well known to those of us who specialize in witchy lore."

This was all news to me. "So, she was a witch?"

That question got me an emphatic headshake. "Oh, no. She was someone interested in the paranormal. I think she started out as a history professor at Boston University, but some of her research had her digging up supernatural bits and pieces, and she sort of veered off in that direction. In fact, I'd heard recently that the university encouraged her to take early retirement rather than face a lengthy battle over losing her tenure."

Again, nothing I'd ever heard about before, but I had to admit that I tended to let the older witches in my coven—or the witch world in general—deal with the people who were interested in the paranormal and sometimes got a little too close to the truth about the witches who hid in plain sight in the modern world. Between running the store and working with the occasional familiar who needed my help, I had enough on my plate.

"Do you think a witch killed her?" I asked, adding, "I mean, because she was about to expose us?"

"I suppose that's one possibility," Grace said, although the way her mouth pursed as she spoke told me she didn't want to entertain the idea. With Halloween fast approaching, today she wore a bright orange sweater with a cat wearing a witch hat knitted into the design, along with orange pumpkin earrings. No, she hadn't gone so far as to dye an orange streak into her graying blonde hair, but no one could have ever accused her of not getting into the spirit of the season. "I hate to think of a witch engaging in that kind of violence, though. And really, we tend to be much subtler than that. A simple forgetting spell would have taken care of the problem if Eunice Bartlett had simply stumbled across concrete evidence that witches do exist."

Grace had a point there. Murdering someone in cold blood like that would draw the attention of the authorities, and we were all about maintaining a low profile. Also, it wasn't as if Eunice had been another witch, and therefore someone who would have posed any kind of a threat to a worker of magic. Any number of simple spells could have ensured she never spoke about her findings...whatever they might have been.

"Does she have any family?" I asked then. Maybe that wasn't really important to the case, but I hated the thought of someone alone in the world dying such a terrible, solitary death.

A pause as Grace stopped to ponder my question. "I'm not sure. I half-remember someone mentioning once that she had a son, but honestly, I can't say for certain."

Well, I supposed that was something I could ask Derek about...if I was given the opportunity. While I didn't think it would be a very good idea to go to him directly, there was always the chance that he'd decide to swing by the shop to ask Sage and me a few more questions.

Recalling the way his eyes had met mine not a half-hour before, I thought it was a pretty damn good chance.

"If she had found something important, I'm

going to assume whatever it was died with her," I said. "All we can do is hope the police figure out who had the motive and the opportunity to kill her."

"Exactly," Grace said with a sad nod. I wondered if she was thinking about her own family, her daughter and son-in-law and grand-daughter...and grandbaby number two on the way. She was around the same age as Eunice Bartlett, but she definitely hadn't lived a solitary life. Then her expression grew brisk, and she said, "But you also wanted to talk to me about runes."

"I did," I replied. "Were you able to find any instances where a familiar suddenly started using an alternate form of communication the way Edgar has?"

She reached for her glass of water and took a sip. "Not so far. The situation seems to be unprecedented. As for the runes themselves, well, they're an ancient form of divination, far older than the Tarot as we know it. I spent some time studying runes this afternoon, but I can't say I'm anything close to an expert. Each stone has its own meaning, although those meanings are very open to interpretation, depending on the person doing the reading and the combination of stones that have been thrown."

Pretty much what I'd already known, and I had to keep myself from frowning. "So why in the world would Edgar start using them to communicate?"

"I have no idea," Grace replied. "The interesting thing, though, is that sets of rune stones sometimes come with a blank stone, one that's referred to as Odin's stone, since it is meant to imply something that can't be known by mere mortals. Also, a pair of ravens named Huginn and Muninn were Odin's companions and flew all over the world collecting information for him. Maybe it's just a coincidence that Edgar started using rune stones for some reason...but maybe there's something else going on here."

I couldn't quite hold back a smile. "What...you think a Norse god is involved in all this?"

Grace, however, maintained her serious expression. "Not exactly. But I think there may be some kind of connection that neither of us can see right now."

I hadn't lingered at Grace's house, not when I knew I was running almost a half-hour behind and that Milo and Lexi and Edgar were probably getting worried. At least I had one of the lamps in the living room on a timer so they hadn't been left alone completely in the dark, but still, I didn't want them to think they'd been abandoned.

Sure enough, the dogs ran up to me the second I entered the room.

"What took you so long?" Milo asked as I reached down to give him a reassuring scratch behind the ears, followed by another one for Lexi. Thanks to the one table lamp illuminating the space, I could see that Edgar had made a nest of his blanket on the sofa and was still curled up there.

"Something came up at the shop," I said, then hesitated. Should I tell them about Sage's discovery of Eunice Bartlett's body? After all, it wasn't as if the dogs had known her.

But I'd decided a while back that it wasn't a good idea to keep things from them, even if the truth might be unpleasant.

"A tragedy," I went on. "Sage found a woman's body by the dumpster behind the store, so we had to stay for a while and talk to the police."

Lexi's big dark brown eyes went even wider with alarm. "A body?" she repeated.

"No one any of us knew," I assured her. "It sounds like a random act of violence. The police are working on it."

This explanation didn't seem to reassure either of the dogs, because Milo said, "I don't like the idea of you going to work there if it's so unsafe."

I paused to send a quick look toward Edgar where he apparently still slept in his blanket on the couch. He hadn't stirred, telling me he didn't seem to have missed me very much.

"He's fine," Lexi put in. "We helped him push his little rocks around this afternoon, but after that, he seemed tired and went to sleep."

Did that mean the raven had been trying to communicate with the two dogs? If so, he would have been doomed to frustration, since Milo and Lexi didn't know any more about runes than I did.

But because Milo was still staring at me, clearly expecting a reply, I said, "The store is safe, and so is that whole neighborhood. This was an isolated incident. I'm sure once the police really get into the investigation, they'll find the motive was personal."

Even as I spoke, however, I couldn't help wondering about that. Who in the world would have a reason to kill a woman in her early sixties, a retired history professor? True, she'd been poking around in the paranormal, according to what Grace had told me, but still, I couldn't begin to imagine what had compelled the murderer to sneak up on her and club her on the head.

Or whatever had happened. Derek hadn't gone into a lot of details, but there hadn't been much blood at the scene, so she hadn't been stabbed. And obviously, the killer hadn't used a gun, or we all would have heard it.

Unless he'd used a silencer, I supposed.

If the killer was even male. Statistics proved

that men committed murder far more often than women did, but still, I knew I shouldn't be jumping to conclusions.

Milo sniffed, and I could tell he wasn't convinced by my arguments. Honestly, I didn't know whether I was, either.

What I did know was that the hour was inching past seven, and that meant I needed to get all of us fed.

"Well, I have the next two days off, so we won't have to worry about how safe the store is until Tuesday," I said, trying my best to sound upbeat. "So, let's go wrangle some dinner."

The next morning, my mother called. I supposed it was inevitable; no way of knowing who had told her what had gone down behind Full Moon Apothecary the evening before, although my suspicions fell on Grace. Then again, Sage's mom, Izzy Halloran, had probably heard the story from her daughter, and it seemed equally likely that Izzy had reached out to my mother.

Izzy was a huge gossip, after all.

"There's not much to say," I told my mother in response to her worried question. "Grace Bowersby had heard of the victim, a woman named Eunice Bartlett. But I don't know what Eunice was doing behind my store, and I certainly have no idea why anyone would have wanted to kill her. I'm not even sure how they managed it, since we had people coming and going from the shop right up until closing, and I assume some of them must have been parked out back."

"It gets pretty dark out there," my mother returned. Her tone bordered on judge-y without quite entering the territory. "I always thought you should install a flood light on your exterior wall out back, just like they have at the candle store."

"The one behind the candle store lights up most of the area involved," I said. "If I put a second one out there, it's going to look like the high school's football stadium at halftime."

Not that I'd spent much of my youth hanging out at football games. However, I'd attended the homecoming game my senior year just because it seemed like the thing to do...even though I bailed out during halftime because I was bored out of my mind.

"I'm sure Eunice was in Salem to stir up some kind of trouble," my mother went on. "Grace told me that she heard from the coven in Ipswich that she was snooping around there a month ago. They even had to move their equinox celebration out of the birch grove where they'd been having it for decades."

Grace hadn't mentioned anything about that

the night before, although I supposed it was possible that she'd started talking to people on her network right after I left and had gathered some new information.

"I'm surprised they'd do something like that in public at all," I remarked. "I mean, we always have our observances in people's basements because it's safer that way."

My mother made a noncommittal sound, but then said, "Yes, but everything in Salem is more public because of all the tourists we have here. No one has disturbed that birch grove in Ipswich for years. Honestly, I'm not sure how Eunice Bartlett even heard about it, although I suppose it's possible that she picked up on a few rumors and went to investigate for herself."

"So, you think one of the Ipswich witches killed Eunice?"

"Of course not," my mother replied, her tone indignant. I'd pretty much anticipated that sort of reaction, so I wasn't too surprised. "Witches don't need to kill people who get too close. You know we can simply cast a go-away spell or a forgetting spell."

Which was about what Grace had said the night before. Still, if Eunice really had been sticking her nose where it didn't belong, it didn't seem too implausible to me that someone from the Ipswich coven might have decided to do something about it. Yes, a spell could have taken care of the problem, but at the same time, spells had been known to fail.

Death was a lot more final.

But since I didn't want to start an argument on the moral turpitude of the Ipswich witches...especially since I barely knew any of them...I decided to let it go.

"No, the killer probably doesn't have anything to do with the coven over there," I said. "So I guess we'll just have to wait and see what the police come up with."

"Who's the detective assigned to the case?" my mother asked, her tone altering subtly.

Like I couldn't see right through that ploy. She might not have been badgering me to get back out in the dating pool, but if she thought fate had dropped Derek Falco right into my lap....

"Detective Falco," I said crisply. "And I'm sure you knew that already. But because I had very little to do with the murder, I doubt he'll need to talk to me about it any more than he already has. Anyway, I need to go—I've got a lot of restocks I need to make today and tomorrow before we open again on Tuesday."

Nothing more than the truth, although I could tell from the extended hesitation on the other end of the line that my mother was deciding whether she should push the issue further or whether she should let it go.

It seemed she'd decided on the latter, because she said, "Then I won't keep you. Enjoy your time off."

And she ended the call there. I set down my phone and allowed myself a small sigh.

Time off? Not really.

But since those bottles of arthritis elixir and sleep tincture weren't going to brew themselves, I knew I needed to get to work.

Chapter 5

The Truth Is Out There

All my time over the next two days wasn't just spent brewing philters and elixirs. No, I made myself sit down with Edgar and try to get some information out of him about his sudden preference for speaking through rune stones, but I didn't have much success. He used the "communication" rune several times, which made sense, although I thought it seemed obvious enough that Sally Hawkins' worries about him had everything to do with the way he wouldn't talk like a normal familiar. The stone's meaning when it was reversed included deceit and misunderstandings, possibly even manipulation, but that still made the whole thing pretty much clear as something written in Egyptian hieroglyphics. Even if some outside force was manipulating Edgar, making him incapable of the kind of communication his mistress might have expected, the stones hadn't provided any insight into who might have been doing such a terrible thing.

But at least on Sunday the weather was fine enough that the two dogs and the raven spent a lot of time outside, keeping them out from underfoot —and also appearing to lift all their spirits. I could tell that Milo and Lexi were doing their best to be kind to Edgar, and since Lexi wasn't a familiar herself, but a dog who'd had a spell cast on her to make her talk, she seemed to have a better idea than Milo of the sorts of things that would cheer up our feathered guest, whether that was inviting him to try a taste of the cheese I'd put out for them or locating a shiny lump of quartz in the garden and showing it to him so he could add it to the cache he kept in his blanket.

I didn't hear from Derek at all that day...not that I'd expected to. As I'd told my mother, I was peripheral to the case at best. Sage was the one who'd found Eunice Bartlett's body, not me. No, the crime might have taken place behind my store, but because I hadn't seen or heard a single thing, I didn't have much to contribute to the investigation.

And I was just fine with that.

On Monday a storm rolled in off the Atlantic, and everything was dreary and gray. However, I did what I could to keep my animal charges cheered up, including playing ball in the living room—an activity that made Edgar excited enough that his frenzied flapping almost knocked over a floor lamp —and making a batch of beef stew so everyone would be able to get some choice morsels when we sat down to dinner that night. Or rather, I sat down while Lexi and Milo kept watch on either side of my chair and Edgar perched on the back of the seat that faced mine.

The scene would probably have been amusing to outside observers, but I didn't find myself particularly amused. Yes, it was great to have my animal companions with me, and yet I couldn't stop thinking about the empty chair next to the spot where I sat, the one Noah would have occupied if he'd been here. Was he also sitting at a lonely table and listening to the rain beat against the windows while wondering if he could have done something differently?

Somehow, I doubted it. That is, while I hadn't heard even a single rumor that he'd started dating again, I also doubted he was beating himself up too much about our split. In his mind, he was the injured party...and I couldn't really argue with that interpretation of the situation. Generations of tradition had prevented me from speaking up, but if I'd told him the truth about me...if I'd had the courage to let him know I was a witch, the latest in a long line of Hughes witches...then maybe I wouldn't be sitting here missing him more than ever.

Done was done, though. Over the centuries, more than one witch had attempted to come up with a spell that could turn back the clock so it would be possible to go back in time and alter one crucial moment, but no one had ever managed to accomplish such a complicated feat.

Instead, I ate as much of the stew as I could manage, then packaged up the remainder—enough to keep me fed for most of the week—and settled down to watch TV with Milo and Lexi and Edgar. The dogs preferred *Animal Planet* to anything else, but I wasn't in the mood for that tonight. Since they were also okay with home improvement shows...probably because the homeowners often had pets...I turned on *Farmhouse Fixer* on HGTV. If nothing else, it might give me a few ideas for sprucing up the house. More than once I'd thought about adding on so I could expand the decidedly cramped living room, but the money and hassle involved had always stopped me.

I kind of doubted a remodel was in my future, and yet I gave myself permission to daydream. If nothing else, pondering an upgrade to my old house might help to keep my mind off Noah Jenkins...or the conundrum of who had sneaked up on Eunice Bartlett and smashed her head in behind the dumpster.

The operative word being "might."

The storm had blown itself out by the time I got up the next morning, so at least I wasn't greeted with more gray skies. Milo and Lexi happily bounded into the yard as soon as I opened the door for them, and Edgar took wing as well so he could fly far above the house and stretch his muscles.

While they were occupied outside, I made myself some coffee, then fetched a couple of empty boxes from the walk-in pantry so I could load up all the various elixirs and tinctures and philters I'd made the past couple of days. With any luck, the restock would be enough to see me through Halloween, now looming in just two days. Experience had taught me that people still tended to hang around on All Saints Day, and even longer if the holiday fell in the middle of the week like it did this year, but things should still be a lot quieter after the day itself.

Breakfast was toast and bacon, and then I told the animals I needed to get to work but should be home at the usual time. Milo looked skeptical, but he didn't say anything, probably because he knew I did my best to be punctual. It wasn't as if I'd planned to have someone murdered behind the store Saturday evening. Also, today I didn't have to worry about stopping by Grace Bowersby's house. She'd told me she would keep researching rune stones—and I had a feeling she was also trying to investigate Eunice Bartlett as best she could—but I knew I wouldn't hear from her unless she'd found something substantive.

I gave myself extra time to drive to the shop, just because I knew the crowds would get worse and worse the closer we got to Halloween. Also, even though I generally didn't plan to arrive at work until a quarter before the hour, I thought it was probably a good idea to be as early as I could manage.

To my relief, no one had taken either of our parking spaces, even though I hadn't refreshed my spell...probably because it was only nine thirty-five, and none of the stores in my block opened until ten. I pulled into my spot and got out, then unlocked the back door so I could fetch a dolly from the stock room and wheel in all the new potions. When I went back out to lock up my Discovery, though, a thought occurred to me.

By the power of space and place,
A cone shall stand in this small space.
To guard this spot and hold it dear,
No car shall park, the path is clear!

. . .

"Should have done that yesterday," I murmured, and satisfied, I headed back into the store.

True, I wouldn't put it past a particularly over-zealous tourist to get out and move the traffic cone I'd just conjured, but I'd deal with that eventuality if and when it happened.

I spent the next ten minutes or so arranging all the new potions on their various shelves. The simple reality of there being space for the majority of them seemed to prove how depleted my stock had gotten, because I ended up only having to store a rough dozen or so bottles in the stock room once I was done.

Just as I was heading back out to the front counter, someone knocked on the glass set into the door. A quick glance over my shoulder told me it was still ten minutes before the hour. Sage should have been here by now, but she wouldn't have knocked, would have instead come in through the back the way she always did.

Frowning, I headed toward the door. This wouldn't be the first time someone had been impatient to get into the shop, but I really wasn't in the mood this morning. No, I wanted as much peace and quiet as possible before I had to deal with any customers.

The person waiting outside was a man, tall and dark-haired. For just a second, I wondered if it was Derek Falco coming back to ask more questions, but as soon as the person shifted so they could peer inside the glass, I could tell this wasn't Derek. The stranger was even taller, and his nearly black hair had light brushes of gray at the temples.

Pushing back my impatience, I paused just inside the door and lifted an arm so I could point at my watch. *Not open yet,* I mouthed.

He shook his head. "I need to speak with you," he said, voice muffled by the door but still audible. "It's about Eunice Bartlett."

I felt my frown deepen. Was this man with the Salem police? He didn't look at all familiar, but I'd be the first to admit that it wasn't as though I was intimately acquainted with everyone on the force.

"Are you working on the investigation?"

"Not exactly," the stranger said. "I'm a colleague of Dr. Bartlett's. My name is Dr. Malcolm Grimes."

Almost at once, my spine stiffened. No, I'd never seen the man in person, but he was another history professor slash paranormal researcher—although affiliated with Roxbury, not Boston University—who had been poking around Salem for at least the last seven or eight years, doing his best to see if he could find anything to support his theory that there might be some real witches hidden among all the pretend ones who worked in the local shops and restaurants. The covens here presented far too much of a unified front for him to get any traction, but still, the last thing I needed right now was to have him turn up on my doorstep.

Of course, I could tell him to go away...but since I was due to open in less than ten minutes, there wasn't much I could do to prevent him from returning and forcing the issue once the doors were unlocked.

Besides, Sage would be here soon enough if I needed backup. Probably better to go ahead and let him in...and hope I could get rid of him before the expected hordes of customers descended.

"Just a minute," I told him, then headed over to the cash register so I could fetch the key and open the door.

Once he was inside, he said, "Thank you," and sent a swift glance around the shop. I didn't know what he was expecting to see, as I knew he'd visited Full Moon Apothecary not too long after I'd opened the place, and not much had changed materially about the store since then.

"Were you working with Eunice?" I asked, doing my best to be polite. No, I wasn't thrilled that he'd turned up like this, but if he'd known the other professor, he must have been trying his best to deal with her loss.

His gaze sharpened—his eyes were nearly as dark as his hair, partially hidden behind a pair of rimless glasses—but then he shook his head.

"Barri? No, I suppose you could think of us more as professional rivals, since we both specialize in paranormal history."

"'Barri'?" I repeated, not sure I'd heard him correctly.

That question earned me a very faint smile. Unlike Eunice Bartlett, who had been in her early sixties, Malcolm Grimes was probably forty at the most, despite the touches of gray at his temples that I'd noted earlier.

"Dr. Bartlett disliked her given name. She was named after a grandmother, I think. She preferred that her friends call her Barri...you know, short for 'Bartlett.'"

I supposed that made some sense. Honestly, I'd kind of wondered how anyone from Eunice's generation had been given that name, since it seemed as though it had gone out of vogue back when Model Ts were popular and she'd been much younger than that.

It was on the tip of my tongue to ask Malcolm Grimes what the heck he was doing poking around the crime scene...or at least, its near vicinity...when he hadn't even been working with Dr. Bartlett. However, that sort of question would have sounded extremely rude, so I said, "I honestly don't know how much I can tell you. My assistant Sage is the one who stumbled across the crime scene, but neither of us really saw or heard anything. You'd do better to talk to the police."

"Oh, I'm not investigating Barri's death," Dr. Grimes replied. "Rather, I'm trying to discover what she was investigating when she was killed. You see, we've both been working under the hypothesis that actual witches are operating here in Salem right under everyone's noses."

It took every ounce of will I possessed to widen my eyes and assume what I hoped was an appropriately astonished expression. "Actual...witches?" I said, thinking my tone was an excellent combination of surprise and skepticism.

Would a chuckle be too much?

Probably, because I wasn't sure I'd be able to fake that as well as the dubiously startled look I knew I wore. Before Malcolm Grimes could reply, I went on, "I think people have been trying to do that for hundreds of years. There aren't any witches here, though...just a lot of people who like to play dress-up."

He didn't smile. His features were angular but not unattractive, although my taste definitely ran to nicely muscled veterinarians with eyes the perfect blue of a summer sky.

"That's the whole point, though, isn't it?" he returned, even as his gaze moved across the orderly shelves of tinctures and elixirs, the display of dried herbs in their small cellophane pouches and printed labels. "To do whatever they can not to attract attention?"

"It's a lot of people playing at witchcraft, that's all," I said. "The tourists just eat it up."

Rather than reply immediately, he stepped closer to the counter so he could read the labels on the bottles displayed directly behind it. "And what exactly do you sell here, Ms. Hughes? Those certainly look like potions to me."

I could feel my lips tighten, but I did my best to sound unconcerned as I said, "Holistic medicine, Dr. Grimes. Folk cures. They work, but there's nothing magical about them...unless you want to count the centuries of tradition that went into their recipes."

Of course, that wasn't the complete truth. While I did lean heavily on folk and traditional medicine for the components of my cures, part of the reason they were so effective was that I also worked various spells as I was concocting them, simple enchantments to ensure they did what they were supposed to do. No, I didn't sell cures for cancer, because doing so would have invited far too much scrutiny of my business and myself by extension, but if you bought a bottle of my insomnia elixir, you'd be ensured sweet dreams until it ran out.

"And it's Charity," I added. "We don't stand on ceremony around here."

Now he did smile...only a little, but enough that he looked a lot more relaxed. "Then neither will I," he replied. "Possibly, it seems a little odd for me to be dropping by like this, but I'd gotten the impression that Barri was on the trail of something big, and then when she was killed so suddenly...." He let the words trail off, although it wasn't too hard to follow his line of reasoning.

Eunice Bartlett had uncovered some sort of evidence that might have vindicated her witch research...or at least, she'd thought she had.

And someone had killed her over it.

I tried to tell myself I was reaching on this one, especially since I certainly didn't have any concrete evidence to back up that theory—and I kind of doubted Malcolm Grimes did, either.

Doing my best to keep my tone light, I said, "I find it hard to believe she found anything terribly interesting out by our dumpster."

"Possibly not," Malcolm allowed. "At the same time, I hope you won't mind if I take a look around."

"Go right ahead," I replied, glad that at least that request was easy enough to grant. "But I doubt you'll find anything. The detective and the deputies who investigated the crime scene were pretty thorough."

Malcolm didn't look dismayed by that

prospect. No, he just said, "And if so, then I'll scratch that possibility off my list."

Well, if he was poking around out back, he wouldn't be in here giving my shelves of potions the hairy eyeball. "This way," I told him, and led him through the stock room and out the rear entrance of the store. To be honest, he could have gone there directly without even requiring my assistance, since the dumpster was located to the side of a public parking lot. However, I got the feeling that he'd wanted to talk to me first, maybe to sound me out on the situation...or maybe just to see whether my store had gotten more incriminatingly witchy in the years since he'd been in here last.

But he headed over to the dumpster after murmuring a brief "thank you," and I went back inside, glad that it had been so easy to distract him.

Good timing, too, because the clock ticked over to ten just as I approached the front door, keys in hand. Several people were already waiting outside, and I told them "good morning" as they came inside and began perusing the various wares on the shelves and the display racks.

Where the heck was Sage, though? She was usually pretty punctual, and it wasn't like her to be this late without texting me to let me know she was running behind.

She came in a few minutes later, breathless, expression apologetic.

"Sorry about that," she said. "Traffic was just awful. Thanks for the traffic cone."

"Oh, right," I said, belatedly remembering the cone I'd conjured into her parking space so someone else wouldn't snag it. "I hope it helped."

"It did," she replied, now smiling a little. However, her expression turned more serious as she added, "Did you know some strange guy is poking around the dumpster out back? I thought the police were done with the crime scene."

"They are," I said. "That's Malcolm Grimes. He's a professor and paranormal investigator."

Sage's nose wrinkled. Judging by her expression of annoyance, I could tell that her mother had probably given her the skinny on Dr. Grimes some time ago...and no doubt had instructed her to give him a wide berth if he showed up in Salem.

"What's he doing with the dumpster?"

I couldn't reply right away, since one of our customers—a thin, stressed-looking woman in her fifties—had come up to the cash register with several bags of herbs and I had to pause the conversation while I handled the transaction. After she left, though, I was able to belatedly reply, "I guess he thinks the murder victim discovered something. What, I have no idea, and I don't know what the heck he thinks he's going to find. If there was any evidence left at the scene, then the police would have found it."

Sage nodded, although she didn't look utterly convinced by my argument. True, Salem was a smallish city with not a lot of crime, and I could see why the deputies on our police force might not have been quite as skilled as the ones with the Boston P.D. or those who worked in other big cities.

She didn't have time to comment, though, because another group of customers came in right then, asking questions about the various elixirs and tinctures we offered. That was fine, though—the mundane activity kept me occupied, and so much time elapsed that I was certain Malcolm Grimes must have given up and headed back to his hotel.

If he was even staying here at all. Trying to get accommodations in Salem at this time of year was near-impossible, and I thought it most likely that he was commuting from Boston, which was only a drive of around an hour each way.

But no, he reappeared about twenty minutes or so after I'd left him out back. His expression was triumphant, and I couldn't help shooting a quizzical glance in his direction as he approached the counter.

He held out a hand. On his palm lay a chunk of sparkling pyrite, almost identical to the one Edgar currently had stashed in his blanket back at my house.

"Do you want to tell me what this is?"

Chapter 6

Fool's Gold

L uckily, the early rush of customers had subsided somewhat, and no one else was nearby, since Sage was over at the herb display explaining how all of our offerings were organic and sustainably sourced.

I looked up from the chunk of rock on Malcolm Grimes' outstretched hand and said, hoping I looked completely guileless and not as though I was doing my best to hide my shock at seeing a crystal nearly identical to the one my raven charge had stashed in his blanket, "Um...iron pyrite. Fool's gold, right?"

"Yes, that's its common name," he said. "But it does seem strange that something like this would have been left behind at the scene of the crime."

It was strange, true...and even stranger that

Derek's deputies wouldn't have located the glittering chunk of mineral. "Where did you find it?"

"On the ground under the dumpster," Malcolm replied. "Wedged up against one of the rear wheels. I suppose that could be why the police didn't find it—they would have had to move the dumpster out of the way completely to see that it was hidden under there."

While I hadn't been present for the entirety of the investigation, I couldn't recall the deputies moving the dumpster at all. They'd gotten down on their hands and knees and shone their flashlights under the blocky metal object, but apparently had decided it was too big and bulky to shift from its current location.

Speaking of knees, I could see some smudges on the knees of Malcolm Grimes' jeans, so it seemed he—unlike the deputies—hadn't hesitated to get down there and poke around.

"I don't know if you can call that a clue, though," I said, and one of his brows lifted.

"What makes you say that?"

While I was desperate to put him off the scent, I knew I had to be as casual about this as possible so he wouldn't think I was overly invested in discouraging him from any further investigations.

"Because there's a New Age crystal shop three doors down from here," I explained. "The owner rents her own dumpster, but she sometimes begs space in the one out back if she's had a particularly big shipment and needs to dispose of a lot of packing material. That piece of pyrite is probably something that fell out of one of her boxes and rolled under the dumpster. I don't know if she even noticed it was missing. After all, it's not particularly valuable on its own, right?"

Malcolm's expression grew speculative. "No, not really. At least, not a specimen this size. I suppose I'll have to talk to the owner and see if she can recall a piece of her inventory going missing."

I wasn't sure how well that interview was going to go. Jessica Owens, the owner of Crystal Bridge, wasn't a witch, although she sure liked to pretend she was one. Unlike me—or the other witches in my coven—she went around dressed head to toe in black, flowing dresses and dusters, doing her best to look like a Stevie Nicks impersonator right down to her flowing, wavy blonde hair. And although she cultivated an airy-fairy kind of persona, I knew she was a cutthroat businesswoman who had once marched into my store and told me to my face that I needed to stop offering bags of loose sage because it undercut her business of selling pre-made bundles for people who wanted to smudge their houses.

Then again, if Malcolm fell for her act, he could waste his time hunting down fake witches while I did my best to get to the bottom of who had killed Eunice Bartlett.

Was it the same person who'd taken away Edgar's ability to communicate easily? And if so, why?

No, there probably wasn't a connection at all. That piece of pyrite had just thrown me off a little.

"The owner's name is Jessica Owens," I said, figuring I might as well do my best to maintain a façade of trying to help.

"Thank you," Malcolm replied. "I'll go see what I can find out."

He deposited the lump of pyrite in his jacket pocket and headed out. Sage came up to the cash register with the customer she'd been helping, and had to wait until the transaction was done and the woman had gone back outside to ask the questions I'd already seen dancing in her eyes.

"How'd you manage to get rid of him?" she asked. "My mom told me once to never let him start a conversation because he's like a dog with a bone."

"Something else distracted him," I replied. "He went off to talk to Jessica."

Sage's mouth twisted. "Good luck with that," she said dryly.

Exactly what I'd been thinking.

The next hour went smoothly enough, with plenty of customers to keep Sage and me busy without things being absolutely crazy. As noon rolled around, I began to think that I'd effectively gotten rid of Malcolm Grimes...

...only to have him stroll back in a few minutes before twelve. He didn't look too annoyed, making me wonder if Jessica Owens had suddenly mellowed out, or whether she'd decided she wanted to play nice with someone who was moderately attractive and only a few years younger than she was.

"Oh, hi," I said. "Any luck with Jessica?"

"Not really," Malcolm replied. "That is, she couldn't remember a stone like that going missing, but she said she supposed it was possible." He paused there, an amused light flickering in his dark eyes. "She tried to cast a spell on the stone I found to discover exactly where it had come from, but obviously, that didn't work."

"Why not?" I asked, knowing how disingenuous the question was.

His gaze met mine. "Because she's not a witch."

I couldn't help grinning. "That's not what she says."

"Well, of course she advertises that she's a witch —it's good for business, isn't it? But it's obvious she has no magical abilities whatsoever. She talks a good game, but neither I nor anyone else has ever seen her cast a truly verifiable spell." Malcolm paused there, looking down at me. I couldn't help worrying that somehow he'd guessed at the secret I'd been hiding, even though I'd done my very best to ensure no one except the other witches in town knew the truth about me.

The next words out of his mouth were completely unexpected...and almost as frightening as a direct accusation that I was a witch.

"Are you free for lunch?"

I blinked at him. "'Lunch'?" I repeated stupidly.

A corner of his mouth twitched. "Yes, lunch. The meal people eat in the middle of the day."

A helpless glance in Sage's direction told me she wasn't about to come to my rescue. No, she just stood a few feet away, looking hugely amused.

"I don't know," I said quickly. "It's a really busy week around here, and I can't take off for very long."

"Sure you can," Sage chimed in, forest-hued eyes full of glee. "I can hold down the fort here. Just try not to take more than an hour."

Right then, I was regretting the big raise I'd given her a few months earlier. However, ramping up my protests would have been too conspicuous, so I said, "Okay, sure. But let's go someplace where we can walk."

"I was thinking the Old Ship," Malcolm said,

naming an English-style restaurant and pub only a block away.

Bowing to the inevitable, I said, "Sounds good. Let me get my purse."

And I hurried back to the stock room to fetch the item in question—even as I sent Sage a dagger of a glance as I went. She might have found the situation hilarious, but I sure as hell wasn't amused.

I was actually surprised we were able to get seated at all, the restaurant was so packed, but the hostess guided Malcolm and me to a table way in the back, tucked into a corner that felt far too private for my liking. However, I did my best to act casual as I accepted a menu and settled my napkin in my lap.

Malcolm didn't seem awkward at all as he scanned the bill of fare briefly before setting it aside. "Have you been here before?"

I couldn't help smiling. "I was born in Salem," I told him. "I don't think there's a single restaurant here that I haven't tried. But I'll admit I don't come here too often, just because I rarely have a sit-down kind of lunch. Usually, I brown-bag it, or Sage and I grab sandwiches from the shop down on the corner."

There—that sounded utterly prosy and kind of

dull. With any luck, I'd be able to bore Malcolm Grimes into believing there was no way in the world I could be a witch.

He didn't seem too dissuaded, though, because he said, "I can understand that. I rarely leave campus for lunch myself."

Which sort of begged the question as to how he'd been able to take off in the middle of a work week to come poking around Salem. Maybe his students were fine with getting an unexpected free day, but I had to believe the head of his department might have a different view of the situation.

Something of what I'd been thinking must have showed in my face, because he added, "I don't teach classes on Tuesdays and Thursdays, which is why I was free to come up here today."

All right, I supposed that made some sense. During my final semester in college, I had an awesome schedule where I only had classes from nine to noon on Mondays, Wednesdays, and Fridays, so I could see how Malcolm might have been able to structure his schedule to give him enough free time for his extracurricular research.

Not that I wanted him to have that much spare time. I didn't believe in the devil, but I could still see how idle hands could lead to all sorts of mischief.

Before I could reply, our server came up to explain the lunch specials and take our orders.

Malcolm and I both asked for fish and chips, although he requested an iced tea while I said I was fine with just water. As jumpy as I was feeling around him, the last thing I needed was a bunch of caffeine bouncing around in my system.

"The piece of iron pyrite has to be a clue," he went on, once the waitress was safely away. "I'm just not sure what it's trying to tell us."

I thought I did know...or at least, I couldn't ignore how much it looked like the one Edgar had back at my house. Why it had ended up near the place where Eunice Bartlett had been murdered, though, I had absolutely no idea.

"In crystal lore, pyrite is a stone associated with abundance," I said. "That's why a lot of people who do those sorts of rituals include it on their altars. Was Eunice into that kind of stuff? That could be why she had some on her, and it fell out of her pocket when she was assaulted."

Malcolm steepled his fingers and tapped them against his chin. He looked so professorial in that moment that I wanted to chuckle.

I kept my amusement to myself, though. Somehow, I didn't think laughing at his appearance was going to earn me any points.

Not that I really wanted to earn points with Malcolm Grimes. No, I just wanted to get this meal over with and head back to the store so I could give

Sage a ration of crap about foisting this lunch on me.

"As far as I know, Eunice didn't subscribe to any New Age beliefs," Malcolm said in response to my question. "She was a pragmatic woman, not given to flights of fancy."

"Except for believing witches are real," I said.

He sent me another of those very direct looks. I didn't doubt that his students probably wanted to shrivel when being skewered by a stare like that, but since I didn't have any grades contingent on his approval, I didn't find it too hard to gaze back at him, eyebrows lifted ever so slightly.

Then he smiled. "Except for that," he agreed. "A belief I also share. I think quite a few things are happening under the surface that many people know nothing about."

Considering I knew for a fact that magic and witches were real, I couldn't really argue with his statement. On the other hand, I had to do my best to keep up the pretense that I was a skeptic of the first order.

"Sounds like the basis for one of those paranormal shows on Discovery," I commented, then paused as the waitress came back with our drinks and told us our food would be out in a few more minutes.

Malcolm reached for the straw our waitress had left at the table along with his iced tea and didn't answer right away, focusing instead on removing the paper wrapper and carefully folding it in thirds before he set it back down near his glass. Then he said, "You don't believe that your herbal concoctions work?"

At least there I felt as though I was back on solid ground.

Mostly.

"They work because the herbs in them have been proven over centuries to help with certain ailments," I replied. "There's no magic involved. It's just chemistry."

"A doctor of medicine might not agree with you."

I'd had this same conversation plenty of times before, so I already had all my arguments lined up. "Actually," I said, "recent research into folk medicines shows they're a lot more effective than standard medical science wants to admit. There are plenty of doctors out there who are now using a more holistic type of medicine, one that involves both modern pharmaceuticals and traditional remedies. So again, nothing magical about it."

He didn't say anything for a moment, and instead picked up his iced tea so he could help himself to a sip. "You seem very passionate on the subject."

Maybe I was. I liked knowing that I was helping people, that my "concoctions" allowed a customer to get a decent night's sleep, or to go through a day pain-free thanks to a spoonful of arthritis elixir each night at bedtime. And all right, some subtle magic was involved, but I wasn't about to admit that to Malcolm Grimes.

"I suppose it's a calling," I said. "My mother has an herb garden at the house where I grew up, and I learned about all the various plants when I was young. When I decided to go into business for myself, it just seemed natural to me that I'd open an apothecary shop."

"Something that fits in with the New Age stores and the Tarot readers and all the rest down-town," Malcolm said, although his tone wasn't exactly combative.

No, it was downright friendly and maybe just a little admiring, and that was the last thing I needed right then. My life was complicated enough already, thank you very much.

"Well, I'm not sure about that," I said. "I mean, I'm fairly certain a bottle of my insomnia elixir would help someone out a lot more than a Tarot reading. But I'll be the first to admit that I don't know a lot about it."

Not a complete lie. While I'd used the Tarot on several occasions to provide some guidance I was sorely lacking, it wasn't as though I relied on the cards on a daily or even weekly basis the way some other witches of my acquaintance seemed to.

"But you will admit it's a little more woo-woo than owning a sporting goods store," Nahan commented, and I found myself chuckling.

"Isn't almost anything more woo-woo than a sporting goods store?" I responded, and he laughed as well.

"I suppose you have a point there."

The waitress appeared then with our food, so we went quiet for a minute as we sprinkled vinegar on our fish and poured a little ketchup on our plates for our fries, then started eating. I had to admit the food was very good, even though I generally didn't eat something quite so heavy in the middle of the day. And sure, I supposed I could have ordered a salad, but who wants to eat something like that at an English pub?

"Do you know if Eunice Bartlett had any family?" I asked after I'd had a few bites of fish and chips. It didn't feel right to eat in utter silence, but at the same time, I thought it was probably a good idea to steer the conversation in a direction that, while maybe not completely neutral, also didn't involve witches and whether the wares I sold in my store had any intrinsic magical qualities.

Malcolm had just placed a mouthful of battered cod in his mouth, so I had to wait for him to finish chewing before he could reply. "Barri had a son," he said, confirming what Grace had told me the day before. "I believe he also lives in Boston. So I assume he'll be up here soon to...handle things."

I tried not to wince. Murder was awful no matter how you looked at it, and one of the most terrible parts was how the family left behind had to handle all the minutiae of an unexpected death. No, Eunice Bartlett hadn't been twenty-five years old or anything close to it, but she still could have looked forward to a few more decades on this planet, maybe more. I doubted her son had ever thought he'd have to bury his mother when she was only a couple of years into her sixties.

"Well, I'm glad she had someone to take care of her," I said. "Even though this has to have been a terrible shock for her son."

"And for everyone who knew her," Malcolm replied. Now his expression was somber, and his tone turned thoughtful as he added, "She's been active in the paranormal community for years, and touched a great many lives during her time teaching at Boston University. I'm sure they'll be just as eager as her son to learn who could have done such a terrible thing."

Something I wanted to know as well, just because I couldn't say I liked the idea of having someone walking around Salem who thought it was okay to bludgeon people to death. I had to believe the crime had been personally motivated, but at the same time, I couldn't help thinking about the members of my coven who were around Eunice Bartlett's age, like Grace Bowersby, or even older, like Valerie Monroe. True, they were witches with an arsenal of spells at their disposal, but still, I didn't want to entertain even the slightest notion that they might be at risk from Eunice's assailant.

"I think everyone will want to know," I replied. "Salem is usually such a safe town."

Even as I spoke, I thought of all the murders that had come into my life over the past few months. True, the majority of them had happened elsewhere—the stabbing death of Trevor Miller, Noah's ex-fiancée's boyfriend, had taken place in Salem, but the rest had occurred in other towns— and yet I couldn't help thinking that the world wasn't quite the safe place I'd once believed it to be.

It didn't seem as though Malcolm knew anything about those other murders, because he didn't try to contradict me. Instead, his expression remained serious as he reached for the malt vinegar and sprinkled a bit more on his beer-battered fish.

"I'm sure the Salem police are working over-time on the case. If nothing else, I can't imagine that the optics of having a violent crime like that happen during the town's busiest season are very good."

No, they probably weren't. I hadn't even glanced at my laptop that morning, so I had no idea how much—if anything—of the killing had hit the local papers. If the number of shoppers in my store was any indication, it seemed that either people didn't know what had happened—or they didn't much care, figuring Eunice Bartlett's murder had been an isolated event and nothing that should affect them directly.

"Well, hopefully, I'll hear something soon," I said, and Malcolm's gaze sharpened.

"Are you that much in the loop on the case?"

Oops. I'd spoken without thinking, but of course Malcolm couldn't know that I'd enlisted Derek Falco's aid during a previous investigation... or that the homicide detective might be a bit more inclined to help me simply because he had an interest in me.

"Oh, not really," I said hastily. "I think it's more that because the murder happened basically on my store's back doorstep, he'll want to keep me updated to help settle my nerves."

That explanation must have been plausible enough, because Malcolm tilted his head in acknowledgment before going back to his French fries.

I really needed to watch what I was saying.

The rest of the meal didn't involve any missteps, though, since we chatted about much less fraught topics, like the ongoing Halloween week activities in Salem and the influx of tourists they brought.

Then Malcolm surprised me by saying, "Are you going to the ball on Saturday night?"

I blinked at him. Some years the Halloween masquerade was held the Saturday before the actual holiday, while on other years—this one included—it took place the Saturday after. It capped a week of festivities and sold out every year. I'd gone exactly once, the year after I graduated from college, but had decided it wasn't really for me and that I'd much rather leave the costume-wearing to other people.

"Oh, no," I replied. "It's kind of a touristy thing. Besides, it's been sold out for months."

Malcolm didn't even blink. "I have an extra ticket, if you're interested."

For a second, I just sat there, fork still in one hand, as he held my gaze and I desperately tried to think of the best way to respond.

Had Malcolm Grimes the witchhunter just asked me out on a *date?*

It sure seemed that way.

I blurted, "I don't even have anything to wear."

Great, Charity. Give him a reason to think you might actually entertain the idea if you had the right costume.

"That's not a problem," he said smoothly. "Several of my students are also active in the drama department, and I'm friends with the woman who runs the wardrobe shop. I'm sure she could find something for you."

Well, he had me neatly cornered there. My second excuse would have been that all the local costume stores would either have rented or sold anything worth wearing, but the coffers of the Boston University drama department's wardrobe shop were probably bursting with all kinds of goodies.

And while I had all sorts of logical reasons for turning Malcolm down, it occurred to me that I hadn't done anything fun—something silly and impractical and completely out of character—for longer than I wanted to contemplate.

All right, I didn't have to calculate how long it had been. At least a month...more, really, because while Noah and I had always had a good time doing even the simplest things, whether that was barbecuing in his backyard or making a trip to the local pet store to stock up on food for the dogs, it wasn't as if he'd ever asked me to a masquerade ball.

"Okay," I said, and smiled across the table at my entirely unexpected date.

"Sounds like fun."

Chapter 7

Mean Girls

"Y ou what?" Sage asked, staring at me in disbelief.

"I might have agreed to go to the Halloween ball with Malcolm Grimes," I said.

Her expression seemed to indicate that she thought I'd finally lost my mind. Clearly, while she'd considered it okay for me to have lunch with the man, anything more than that was stepping into dangerous territory. "Isn't he the guy who keeps trying to prove witches are real?"

"Yes," I replied. I hadn't broached the topic until there was a lull in the afternoon's shoppers, so no one was around to hear our convo. "But he asked, and I thought it sounded like fun."

"You hate crowds," Sage pointed out.

Okay, she had me there. It wasn't as if I was a recluse or anything, but in general, I preferred the kind of date where we had dinner at a quiet restaurant and then went home and watched TV. Sharing a ballroom with a thousand-plus people I didn't know—some locals attended, but the Halloween masquerade tended to skew toward tourists— wasn't exactly up my alley.

"Haven't you ever done anything crazy?" I asked, and her face relaxed into a smile.

"Lots of times. I guess I just wasn't expecting it of you."

"Maybe I decided it was time to let my hair down," I said, then paused. "Besides, haven't the whole lot of you been hoping I'd stop brooding about Noah Jenkins and get on with my life?"

Sage didn't reply for a moment, her hesitation telling me that my love life had definitely been a topic of discussion amongst our coven members whenever I wasn't around.

"I think we were worried about you and wanted you to move on when you were ready," she said, her tone uncharacteristically serious. "But I'm pretty sure no one would have told you that Malcolm Grimes was a good person to move on with. I mean, we've all done our best to avoid him, and now you're going on a date with the guy?"

I had to admit that on the surface, the situation was less than optimal.

"I'll be careful," I replied. "It's not like I'm

going to get drunk and blab all our secrets to him or anything."

Sage made a face. "Well, obviously. I know you would never do anything like that."

"Then what's the problem?"

Once again, she paused. Expression turning somber again, she said, "I guess I'm just worried about what might happen if you end up actually liking him."

———

I didn't have much time to brood over my rash decision after that, because the lull abruptly ended and we were flooded with customers from then until the time five-thirty mercifully rolled around and we could close up shop and call it a day.

As I was heading out to my SUV, my cell phone pinged. I scrabbled inside my purse to pull it out, wondering if Malcolm had texted me for some reason. We'd exchanged numbers toward the end of lunch, and I'd made a vague comment about getting together sometime to figure out our costumes, but I honestly hadn't thought I'd hear from him again so soon.

But the text wasn't from Malcolm—or from Derek, who'd been silent all day.

No, Sally Hawkins was the one who'd messaged me.

I just wanted to check on Edgar. Have you made any progress?

At once, guilt washed over me. True, I'd already told her that I'd have to deal with her raven's communication issues around my work schedule, since there was no way I could take any time off during the busiest sales days of the year. Still, I'd been so occupied with the details of Eunice Bartlett's murder—and a little knocked off my stride by Malcolm Grimes' arrival on the scene—that I hadn't spared a lot of mental energy on Edgar's sudden preoccupation with rune stones.

Standing there in the parking lot and texting back a reply seemed silly, so I went ahead and climbed into my Discovery and put on my seatbelt, then picked up my phone again.

Nothing much yet. But I wanted to ask, do you know where Edgar got that piece of pyrite he keeps with his stuff?

The reply came back almost immediately.

No, I don't. I just assumed he picked it up some-where while he was poking around the yard. Why? Do you think it's important?

I honestly didn't know for sure. Pyrite was a fairly common mineral, and since ravens and crows were naturally attracted to bright, shiny objects, it wasn't that strange for Edgar to have some among his stash.

Then again, it was a strange sort of thing to

find at a crime scene, so I couldn't help wondering how the chunk Malcolm had discovered had ended up under that dumpster in the first place.

I don't know. I just thought I should check to see if you knew where it came from.

Sally was probably mystified by that non-response, but her answer was measured enough.

No, Edgar has picked up various bibs and bobs the whole time I've had him. He has his current favorites, and the ones he's not as interested in anymore go into a chest I keep in the guest room.

I supposed she would have to have some means of keeping her raven's little treasures safe even when he abandoned some of them for something new and shiny. After all, I could see how he might want to reclaim one of them if he changed his mind.

How long has he had the pyrite among his favorites?

Sally didn't reply at once, making me think that she probably had to pause and ponder exactly when the shiny hunk of mineral had made its way into his collection.

But then her answer appeared on my phone's screen.

Not long. Maybe a week or so?

Right around the time when he'd started speaking to her with the rune stones. It could all have been a complete coincidence...but I didn't think so.

However, I wasn't going to reveal my suspicions to her, not when I had so little to go on.

Thanks, Sally. I was just about to head home when I got your message, but I need to get going. I don't want to keep the animals waiting.

If she was at all startled by this apparent *non sequitur*, her reply didn't show it.

Then I won't keep you. Give Edgar a hug for me.

I promised her I would, and we ended the conversation there. As I started my Discovery's engine, though, my brain was still racing a mile a minute.

What was it about that piece of pyrite? And why had an almost identical chunk been hiding at the scene of Eunice Bartlett's murder?

It wasn't the first time I had a lot more questions than answers, but I somehow doubted I would be able to puzzle out any of them anytime soon.

At least everything was relentlessly normal at the house—I reheated a bowl of the stew I'd made the night before, fed Lexi and Milo and Edgar and allowed them out into the backyard to get some fresh air before I closed everything down for the night, and then sat down on the couch to put my feet up and digest.

However, my rest and relaxation time didn't last very long, since my phone rang only about fifteen minutes after I'd put my bowl in the dishwasher and settled myself on the living room couch.

My first instinct was to ignore the thing, but I knew I couldn't do that, not when I was watching someone's familiar. True, Edgar had been fairly subdued and hadn't shown any interest in using his rune stones after I lifted the bag and jingled it, signaling that I was ready to talk if he was.

Clearly, he hadn't been in the mood, though, and I decided not to push things. Yes, I realized I couldn't keep him here indefinitely, and at some point would need to probe a little harder, but it had been a very long day.

The home screen on my phone told me it was my mother calling, and the impulse to turn the thing off grew even stronger.

Just get it over with, I told myself. Dealing with my mother was a lot like dealing with a Band-Aid that had been in place too long—better to rip it off and get past the discomfort as quickly as possible.

"Hi, Mom," I said after I touched the screen to accept the call. Hopefully, I didn't sound too resigned.

"Are you really going to the Halloween ball with Malcolm Grimes, of all people?"

Since she couldn't see me, I allowed myself an eye roll. And I wouldn't bother to ask how she'd found out so quickly—I guessed that Sage had mentioned something to her mother, and Izzy Halloran had jumped right on the phone to call my mom.

"I am," I said calmly. "He seems to have mellowed over the past couple of years."

Like a fine wine, kind of. When he'd first popped up in Salem, I hadn't paid any real attention to his appearance, but had only classified him as a somewhat dangerous busybody and left it at that. Now, though, he seemed to have grown into his longish nose and angular features, and even if he was nowhere near as handsome as Noah—really, who was?—he was certainly attractive enough.

Also, Malcolm had seemed shaken by Eunice Bartlett's death, a reaction that humanized him a good deal, made him seem much more like a real person than a man obsessed with proving witches were real.

"Don't be fooled," my mother said darkly.

I sat up straight and reached for the glass of water I had sitting on the coffee table in front of me. As I was heating up my bowl of stew, I'd thought about pouring myself a glass of wine but had decided against it.

Now, though, I kind of wished I had some cabernet in front of me, rather than a plain glass of water.

"Fooled by what?" I returned. "Do you know something I don't know?"

My mother's sigh was audible through the phone's tiny speaker. "No," she said, although I could detect some reluctance in her tone, as if she wished she could tell me she had new evidence regarding Malcolm Grimes' witch-hunting crusade. "He hasn't been here in Salem for at least a year, so it seems as if he's been keeping a low profile. But I just don't think it's a good idea for you to be doing anything with him socially."

"Duly noted," I said. "And it's not like he asked me to marry him or something. He just wants to take me to the Halloween dance. Honestly, you can't get much more public than an event like that, right?"

She didn't reply at once, telling me I'd scored a point with that comment. "Maybe," she allowed. "But still, you'll need to be on your guard every single second you're with him."

Just like I was with everyone on the planet except my fellow witches. Keeping that part of our natures secret from the world was so ingrained in us that I doubted I'd slip up with Malcolm just because he had a personal interest in finding out whether people like us truly existed.

"I will be," I said. "It's okay, Mom. I'm a big girl."

Another pause, and I wondered if she was going to leave it alone or find a new way to drill into me what a stupid idea it was for me to have accepted Malcolm's invitation to the dance.

But this was my mother I was dealing with. She'd never been very good at letting things go.

"I know you took your breakup with Noah very hard," she said, her tone softening. "And I think it's good that you've decided to get back out there. I'm just not sure whether Malcolm Grimes is the person to be doing it with."

"Do you think he's some kind of crazy rebound?" I retorted. "Give me a little credit, Mom. It's just a dance. One date. No big deal."

"A single date can sometimes turn into a lot more."

Well, yes, that was how things were supposed to work, weren't they? You went out for drinks, or maybe dinner and a movie, and then you progressed from there to a visit to a museum or a concert, and from there to maybe a weekend in Cape Cod, and before you knew it, you had a white picket fence and 2.5 kids.

My case, however, was entirely different. I'd never been one to rush things, which was why I'd been as surprised as anyone when I fell for Noah Jenkins so hard—and so quickly.

Maybe that was why it had hurt so much when it ended.

Anyway, even if my heart had gone pitter-pat for Malcolm Grimes the same way it did for Noah...which it didn't...I wasn't going to make that same mistake twice.

"I don't think that's going to happen," I told my mother. "Besides, you know what they say—keep your friends close, but your enemies closer."

I had the distinct impression that she lifted an eyebrow. "Are you saying Malcolm Grimes is your enemy?"

No, he wasn't that. To be honest, I wasn't sure what he was.

Not yet.

"Let's just say I'm approaching him with guarded neutrality," I replied. "And that's where I'm going to leave it. Honestly, it's been a long day and I just want to crash. None of this is a big deal."

"If you say so." A pause, and she added, "Have a good night, Charity. I hope tomorrow things are a little quieter."

So did I.

The next morning, Edgar still didn't seem interested in his rune stones, which bothered me. When I held up the bag, he just stretched his wings and then tucked them close before he settled back down on his blanket, seeming to signal that he thought the interaction was over.

I tried to tell myself it wasn't a big deal. Maybe his lack of interest in the stones was a signal that the spell...or whatever it was...had begun to wear off. If that was the case, then he might be back to talking very soon.

Or he might just be feeling cranky this morning, in which case he wasn't getting better at all.

As best I could, I pushed my worries aside. Right now, it was more important to get everyone's breakfasts ready, including mine. A lot of the time, I was okay with some coffee and toast, but with another grueling day beckoning, I made sure to fortify myself with some bacon and eggs in addition to a slice of sourdough toast. While I was cleaning up afterward, I let Milo and Lexi and Edgar out into the backyard to enjoy the sunshine. The clouds of the day before had cleared up, and the weather promised to be gorgeous, if a bit nippy.

They knew the drill by now, and seemed fine as I waved goodbye and headed out the side door toward the driveway. Once again, I found myself wishing I'd made more progress with Edgar, but I was finding myself more at a loss than I usually was when working with familiars. All those other times, I'd at least been able to talk to the animals involved, but communicating with the rune stones was much more difficult even when he felt inclined to use them.

Well, Sally hadn't pressured me too much about the timing of his possible return, so I knew I shouldn't beat myself up about the situation. Either I'd work it out, or I wouldn't. I hated to admit defeat, though. This would be the first time I'd been properly flummoxed by one of my charges, and it felt wrong to even entertain the thought of handing Edgar back over to his mistress without solving the mystery of the rune stones.

By that point, I was so used to the Halloween week traffic that I barely paid it any notice. No, I just maneuvered my way into my parking space, conjured another traffic cone to secure Sage's spot, and then unlocked the back door and went inside.

I'd purposely come early because I knew the store was going to need some tidying up before we opened at ten. In a way, that was good, because the quiet time allowed me to settle into the energy of the shop, to breathe in the herb-scented air and know that, while the coming day was going to be busy, it was nothing Sage and I couldn't handle.

She was also early, and came in looking vaguely sheepish.

"Sorry my mom spilled everything to your mom," she said as she approached the herb display, where I was hanging a new set of packets.

I couldn't help smiling. "It's fine," I replied. "I

mean, she was going to find out sooner or later. She expressed her disapproval, I told her I was a big girl, and that was the end of that."

Sage looked vaguely awed. "I don't know how you do it," she said. "Deal with your mom, I mean. She's so...intimidating."

That was one word for her, I supposed. It wasn't as if she was rude or difficult to deal with—and clearly, she had a charm that played well on YouTube and Instagram—but she did have a tendency to think that her opinion of something was the be-all and end-all, and everyone should fall in line with it.

"Years of practice," I said lightly.

My assistant grinned, as I'd hoped she would. She also seemed to understand no further apologies were necessary, because she murmured that she wanted to water the plants before we opened for the day. A few months earlier, I'd had Maggie Phillips, who owned a plant design business in Marblehead, come over and place a few strategic specimens around the shop to green it up a little and make it a bit more inviting. While Maggie dropped by once a month to check on everything and make sure the greenery still flourished, Sage had taken it upon herself to water the plants every Wednesday.

I finished tidying up the herb racks, checked the time, and headed over to the cash register so I could retrieve the front door key. Just as I was pulling it out, my phone binged.

A text from Malcolm.

I spoke to Alicia Hoyt, who runs the costume department here at the school. She said you should send her your measurements, and then she'll see what she has in the warehouse that might work for you.

From someone else, it might have felt a little skeevy to be asking for my measurements. However, since Malcolm had provided Alicia's email address and it looked official enough, with a bostonuniversity.edu suffix, I supposed it was all on the up and up. And if we did it this way, I wouldn't have to figure out how I could possibly squeeze in the time to drive down to Boston and try on a bunch of stuff.

I sent him a quick text back, thanking him for Alicia's email and letting him know I'd send her the information sometime today. He responded with a thumbs-up, which seemed to indicate that he felt he'd relayed the message he needed to send and that he didn't see any need to continue the conversation.

Hearts and flowers, he was not. I was fine with that, though. If he'd come on too strong, I would have found myself rethinking my hasty acceptance of his invitation to the Halloween ball. As it was, everything seemed breezy and downright casual, just the way I liked it.

A crowd had already started to gather outside on the sidewalk, but I made myself wait until exactly ten o'clock before I unlocked the door and let everyone in. Immediately, they began fanning out through the store, everyone intent on finding the perfect solution to whatever ailed them—or maybe just curious, since I saw a lot of people only pick up bottles and read the labels before replacing the elixir or tincture in question back on the shelf.

Which was fine. I never wanted anyone to feel pressured into buying something they didn't need, and I'd already grossed enough over the previous couple of weeks that I knew I'd have a nice cushion to get me through the lean months of January and February and March.

All in all, I was feeling pretty good about life in general...except for my continuing failure to identify exactly what was going on with Edgar. However, that mood went crashing into the basement when Jessica Owens walked into the store. Her gaze went immediately to me, and she stalked over to the spot where I stood behind the counter.

Well, more like glided, because those floaty garments she wore always made it look more like she was drifting along carried by an unseen wind, but, judging by the way her light blue eyes wanted to bore into me like laser beams, I could tell she wasn't here merely to chat about strategies for dealing with the town's Halloween crowds.

At least she had the decency to wait until I was done ringing up my current customer before she said, "I want to talk to you."

"About?" I asked.

She glanced around. Patrons still crowded the store, so no one could have called the setting at all private. I had to guess that her shop was similarly busy, but because she had two assistants, she was in a better position to leave whenever she felt like it.

"We should talk somewhere else."

Was she nuts? But I could see the way her jaw had set and knew I probably wouldn't be able to get rid of her until she'd had a chance to speak her piece...whatever it turned out to be.

"All right," I replied, then glanced over at Sage, who had been helping someone with the herb rack but murmured an apology to the woman before heading over to the cash register.

"What's up?"

"Can you keep an eye on things for just a minute? Jessica has something she wants to talk to me about."

Sage's dubious gaze moved to the other woman and then back to me. To my relief, though, she didn't protest, and only said, "Sure, no problem."

With that handled, I tilted my head at Jessica and then began moving toward the stock room, signaling that she should follow. It still wasn't the most private place in the world, but at least there was the Japanese screen I'd set up to conceal the small table where Sage and I usually ate lunch, and I figured that was the best place for Jessica to get whatever it was off her chest.

Once we were safely hidden behind the screen, she crossed her arms and sent me a baleful stare. "He's way too old for you."

"Um...what?" I managed. We'd known each other for years, so it wasn't so much the familiar way she'd addressed me as the fact that I had no idea what the heck she was talking about.

"Malcolm Grimes," she retorted. "You know, the man you had come over and talk to me yesterday? I thought he and I had a real rapport—he gave me his card and everything—but when I called him this morning to see if he was interested in getting lunch, he told me he didn't think it would be appropriate, since he would be seeing someone else later this week."

I wasn't sure how she'd figured out that I was Malcolm's date for Saturday, since it didn't sound to me as if he'd been that specific. Then again, even though we'd had a somewhat secluded table at the Old Ship, we'd had to walk by a whole bunch of tables and booths to get there. It didn't seem too implausible that one of Jessica's friends or acquaintances had seen me at the restaurant with him and might have mentioned it to her.

Still, I didn't think it would hurt to dance around the issue as much as I possibly could.

"Isn't he teaching today?" I pointed out. "I doubt he would have even been available for lunch in Salem."

That comment didn't go over very well, though, because her eyes narrowed and she said, "How would you know what his teaching schedule was?"

"He might have said something when he was over here yesterday, talking to me about Eunice Bartlett's murder."

Any hope that the mention of an innocent woman's violent death might derail Jessica's diatribe disappeared in the next moment as she said, "I doubt that, especially since my friend Tori was waiting on your table and overheard you talking about his days off."

Ah, there was the source of the leak. No wonder Jessica had so much inside information about my connection to Malcolm Grimes.

"How old do *you* think he is?" I asked, genuinely curious.

Her eyes narrowed again. "At least ten years older than you are, which makes him a much better option for me."

Maybe that was true on paper, but if he'd truly been interested in her, she would have been the one he'd asked out for lunch, not me. However, I had a feeling that if I pointed out such an obvious truth, Jessica's mood wouldn't improve very much.

Then again, I doubted anything I said right now would go over very well, and I needed to cut the conversation short before I left Sage alone with all those customers for too long.

"Well, he's a big boy," I said lightly. "And I guess that means he can make his own decisions about his personal life. But now I need to get back to work."

I shifted my weight, signaling that I was about to step past her. She moved as well, effectively blocking me.

"Don't think this is over!" she snapped, and turned on her heel so she could go to the back door and let herself out.

Not really the way I'd wanted to end the conversation, but at least she hadn't told me she was going to meet me back behind the gym at three-thirty to beat me up for stealing the guy she liked.

Complications piled on top of complications, and the week wasn't even half over yet.

Shaking my head, I went back out front.

Chapter 8

Clear as Mud

"**W**hat did *she* want?" Sage asked.

While I would have preferred not to go into detail about Jessica's flounce, it was probably obvious to anyone in a ten-mile radius that she wasn't exactly thrilled with me. Trying to brush it off wouldn't work, especially with someone like my assistant, who'd also been around Jessica Owens long enough that she knew how the other woman generally operated.

"Oh, she's mad that I stole her guy," I remarked, and Sage made a surprised little sound.

"Malcolm?"

"Yes," I said. "Apparently, they had a 'rapport,' and I got in the way of that. But if she thinks the mean-girl act is going to work on me, she's in for a surprise."

"Isn't she older than him?"

I couldn't help smiling. "Probably by a couple of years, but not nearly as much as the gap between his age and mine, as she made sure to point out."

"People are weird," Sage commented, and I couldn't do much except nod in agreement.

Yes, people were weird...mundanes sometimes the most of all.

As my mother liked to say, it never rained but it poured. A little past two, Derek Falco came into the store, and at once Sage shot a significant glance in my direction.

Since I knew my assistant was on Team Derek —well, since it seemed as if Team Noah had been permanently sidelined—I did my best not to respond. Instead, I put on what I hoped was a pleasant smile as Derek came over to the counter, where I'd just finished up a customer's order the moment before.

"Hi, Derek," I said. "What's up?"

"I thought I'd come by and give you an update," he replied. His keen dark eyes seemed to take in each occupant of the shop, as though judging the likelihood of any of them interrupting our conversation. "But it looks like you're kind of busy."

"Oh, I can keep an eye on things," Sage put in

as she walked over toward us. Clearly, she wasn't going to allow me to be deprived of Derek's company if there was anything she could do about it.

With him standing right there, I couldn't really narrow my eyes at her the way I wanted to. Instead, I told myself to act like it wasn't a big deal, saying, "We can talk in the back, if that works."

"Good idea," he replied. "Some of this shouldn't be discussed in public."

Which begged the question as to why he'd driven over here to talk in the first place, rather than asking me to come to his office at the police station. However, he'd probably guessed I couldn't easily get away from the shop, even if he'd misjudged how busy it was.

"This way," I said, and gestured for him to follow me back to the stock room.

Well, if I had to have a second convo back here in as many hours, I much preferred to do so with Derek Falco than Jessica Owens.

"So, there've been developments in the case?" I asked.

"A few," Derek replied. "The medical examiner determined for certain that Eunice Bartlett died of blunt force trauma. What's strange is the fragments he found caught in her hair and her scalp."

"'Fragments'?" I echoed, frowning. "Did the

killer hit her over the head with a bottle or something?"

"Not a bottle. What must have been a fairly large piece of iron pyrite."

My stomach clenched, but somehow I managed to stop myself from gaping at him in shock. "That's a kind of mineral, right?"

"Yes," he replied. "Fool's gold. It fractures easily, which is probably why there were so many small pieces left in Ms. Bartlett's hair. But even though it's fragile, a big enough chunk would have been more than enough to cave in her skull."

I winced, my brain manufacturing the terrible scene despite my best efforts to stop my imagination from spinning it up. A dark figure sneaking up behind Eunice Bartlett...a hand raised, holding the chunk of pyrite...her body slumping to the ground as the attacker ran away.

But why pyrite? Now more than ever, I realized there must be a connection between Edgar's communication problems and Eunice Bartlett's murder, even if I couldn't figure out how, or why.

And the piece of pyrite Malcolm had found under the dumpster must have broken off from the rock when the killer smashed it against Eunice's head, then slid out of the way.

It should have been a significant piece of evidence, but since Malcolm had already picked it up and touched it more than once, any fingerprints that might have remained on the mineral's shiny surface would now be long gone.

Should I mention it anyway?

While I wrestled with that conundrum, Derek went on, "Whoever did it, they must have had some kind of grudge against her. It's way too personal a murder for a robbery. Besides, nothing was taken from her purse—not her phone or credit cards, or the small amount of cash she was carrying. And she was wearing a valuable diamond band."

A wedding ring? From everything I'd heard so far, it sounded as though Eunice Bartlett had been fairly alone in the world, except for her son. But I supposed she could have been widowed or divorced. I had several customers who'd simply moved their anniversary bands to their right hand and stacked them with other rings after their divorce, rather than stop wearing an expensive piece of jewelry altogether.

"But who would want to kill her?" I asked, and Derek shook his head.

"That's what we're working on right now. So far, it doesn't seem as though she had any enemies. From what I've been able to gather, it sounds like her colleagues at Boston University thought she was kind of a crackpot, but a harmless one."

"'Crackpot'?"

Although the topic of our conversation had been grim enough, he smiled then. "I guess she was convinced that witches were real and spent a lot of energy trying to prove her theory. Eventually, the head of her department requested that she take early retirement." Derek paused, reaching up to run a hand through his crisp black hair, mussing it ever so slightly, making him even more devilishly handsome, if possible.

Maybe Sage was right. Maybe I should have tried a little harder to be on Team Derek once it was clear that Noah wasn't coming back.

But then, it wasn't as though Derek had asked me to the Halloween ball, or even out for coffee. And I was way too much of a coward to have made the first move...despite knowing it probably would have been received positively.

"Witches," I said, and essayed a laugh that I hoped sounded natural. "That's kind of crazy, don't you think?"

"Well, that's what Dr. Bartlett's colleagues thought," he replied, even as his smile faded and his tone turned thoughtful. "Otherwise, it seems like a harmless enough hobby to me. There are plenty of people right here in Salem who claim to be witches, so it wasn't like she would have had to look far."

No, you couldn't throw a rock in my home-town without hitting a so-called "witch," even though none of them were true magical practition-ers. Dressing up in a flowing black dress and Victo-rian boots and swanning around town in a pointy hat didn't make you a witch. Either you had magical blood in your veins, or you didn't.

However, I couldn't tell Derek any of that.

"Salem definitely has plenty of witches," I agreed. "And they're all pretty open about it. So I still can't see how Dr. Bartlett's supposed 'hobby' would have had anything to do with her death."

"It probably doesn't," Derek said. "The killer could be a disgruntled student, or a neighbor who got pissed off because she didn't keep her yard tidy."

I stared at him. His expression was serious, although I couldn't help saying, "You're joking, right?"

Still no smile. "You'd be surprised what some murderers use as their motivation to get rid of someone they don't like. I'll admit the neighbor theory is kind of a long shot, but if she derailed some student who was on a Ph.D. track and put their career hopes in the garbage, I could see why that might send someone into a murderous rage."

Since the news was full of people who'd committed violent acts for reasons that often seemed specious at best, I couldn't argue with him on that one. But if the killer really was one of her former students, then they must have waited a while to take their revenge since she wasn't even on the faculty at the college anymore.

I said as much, and Derek only shrugged. "She

retired at the end of June, so it hasn't been that long. The slight would have still been fresh enough that someone might have been motivated to take matters into their own hands."

That timeline made more sense. Or at least, as much sense as any of this made.

"Anyway, that's where we are," he went on. "The more information I get, the more it seems this was definitely a targeted killing and not a random murder, but still, you and Sage should be careful about going out back alone, especially after dark. Lots of strangers in this town at this time of year."

Since I had them coming and going in my shop all day long, I knew that observation was only the truth. Somehow I doubted the people who came into the store to buy arthritis elixirs or anti-inflammatory teas were stone-cold killers, but still, I didn't know any of them, either.

How could anyone truly know what lay behind the smiling face most people presented to the world?

A small shiver ran down my back. "We'll be careful," I promised.

"Then I'll get back to the station," he said. "I've got some more calls I need to make." He paused there, as if to take in my expression a little more closely. "Is everything okay?"

Now or never. Maybe that piece of evidence

had already been destroyed by careless handling... but I also knew I would never forgive myself if I didn't mention it to Derek now.

"I, um—" A breath, and then I said, "There was a piece of pyrite under the dumpster. I didn't know it had anything to do with the case, and Malcolm found it when he looked under there—"

"Malcolm?" Derek cut in, tone sharpening. "Who's that?"

"Dr. Malcolm Grimes," I replied. "He's a professor at Roxbury University—a friend of Eunice's, I guess. He came to talk to me yesterday about her death, and then when he looked more closely under the dumpster, he found the piece of pyrite. I thought it must have come from Jessica Owens' shop, since she sells that kind of stuff and I thought maybe it had rolled under there when she tossed some of her packing material in the dumpster." I paused, then made myself go on despite Derek's deepening frown. "I should have kept it and passed it on to you."

Something of the contrition in my voice must have gotten through to him, because his expression softened at once. "It's not your fault," he said. "My deputies should have found it—they told me they shone their flashlights under the dumpster and didn't see anything, and that was why they didn't move it." His mouth tightened a little as he added, "Clearly, I should have asked them to, but at the time, we hadn't located much physical evidence at the scene, which is why we all thought there wasn't any. The rock you found probably isn't going to help a lot if it's already been handled, but it's still a good idea for you to give it to me, just so I can have the labs check to see if there's anything left on it that might be useful."

Probably his tactful way of telling me there might still be biological residue on the piece of pyrite, maybe skin or hair or blood.

I would have been more than happy to hand it over, except....

"I don't have it," I said. "Malcolm took it with him back to Boston. But I can ask him to bring it back the next time he comes to Salem."

Whenever that was. It sure seemed as if we had a firm date for Saturday night, or I doubted he would have asked me to get in touch with Alicia Hoyt, the drama department's wardrobe mistress, but he hadn't mentioned anything about returning to Salem before then.

Derek was too good a cop to allow too much of what he was thinking to seep through into his expression, but I could tell from the slight tensing of his jaw muscles that he wasn't too thrilled to hear this piece of news.

"No, that's all right," he said. "I'll reach out to Dr. Grimes and arrange to go to Boston to get the specimen from him. Do you have his contact information?"

"Just a sec," I replied. In a way, I was relieved that Derek would be the one to tell Malcolm he needed to hand over the chunk of pyrite. Otherwise, that conversation might have been a little awkward.

Because we were back near the break area, it was easy enough for me to go over to the shelf where I kept my purse, dig out Malcolm's card—he'd given it to me at the end of our lunch—and hand it over to Derek. I already had his phone number stored in my contacts list, so it wasn't as though I needed the card anymore.

"Thanks," Derek said, giving the card a brief look before he stowed it in his jacket pocket. "This will save me some time."

"I'm really sorry about the rock," I replied. "It was stupid of us to keep it."

"Don't worry about it," he said at once. "Like I said, there was no way for you to know it was connected to Eunice Bartlett's murder. But now that the M.E. has determined that a blow from a large piece of the mineral was the cause of death, we'll need to examine it more closely."

He paused there, looking as though he wanted to say something else, but instead, he thanked me again for Malcolm's card and left via the back door.

I watched him go, also wondering if there had

been a moment when I could have offered a few words to make the situation better, then shook my head.

Malcolm and I had made a mistake, that was all.

I just had to hope it wasn't a fatal one.

Sage shot me a curious glance when I came back out front, but because more customers had crowded into the store, she couldn't say anything until there was a break in the action.

"What did he want?"

Although Derek hadn't sworn me to secrecy or anything like that...I had a feeling more stories about Eunice Bartlett's murder would probably hit the local papers soon...I wasn't sure I wanted to give Sage all the details. For one thing, they were kind of grisly, and for another, I knew that anything I told her would get to her mother sooner rather than later, and then it would be all over town.

Besides, knowing the particulars wasn't going to change anything.

"He just wanted to talk to me about Dr. Bartlett's case," I said. "There aren't a lot of new developments, but the cause of death was definitely ruled to be blunt force trauma."

Sage's nose wrinkled. "I thought the police knew that already."

"Well, that's what it looked like at first glance," I replied. "But they couldn't be definite about anything until they had the report from the medical examiner. Now they have that, they can proceed."

"I'm not sure where they're going to proceed," she remarked as the door to the shop opened again and a group of three women, probably in their late forties, entered and looked around with interest. "It doesn't sound like they have a lot to go on."

She had to stop there, because the new arrivals came up to the counter and began peppering us with questions. That was fine by me, though, because it prevented Sage from asking any further probing questions. With any luck, we'd be so busy from now until closing that we wouldn't have the opportunity for further conversation.

That turned out to be the case, and by the time we shooed the last customers out and locked the doors, she seemed to have forgotten about the matter, or at least realized there wasn't much point in pushing further. No, she only wished me a good evening before heading out to her car—to a parking lot that was now extra illuminated, since I'd turned on the light about an hour earlier when I went to get something from the stock room.

I got my purse and hurried out as well, not

wanting to be left alone for too long despite the extra precautions we'd taken. In fact, Sage was backing her Nissan Leaf out of its parking space as I emerged from the rear of the store, and she paused and waited, headlights trained on me, until I'd gotten inside my SUV and locked the doors.

Eunice Bartlett's death might have been an isolated incident, but that didn't mean we were taking any chances.

However, I didn't back out right away. It had been so busy that I hadn't had a chance to scoop my phone out of my purse to see if I had any missed calls or texts.

Of course I had...a single text from Malcolm.

Derek Falco from the Salem police contacted me about the stone we found at the crime scene. Once I realized what had happened, I told him we shouldn't have taken it and that of course I would bring it to him. He said that wasn't necessary, and instead came by a little after four to retrieve it. It was my mistake—I shouldn't have assumed the pyrite had nothing to do with Eunice Bartlett's murder. I hope the detective didn't give you too much trouble over the thing.

Reading this, the knot of worry that had tightened in my stomach immediately relaxed. He wasn't angry with me for siccing the police on him. In fact, he seemed to think the whole mix-up was his fault.

Clearly, Malcolm Grimes was a much nicer guy than I'd initially thought.

The message was time-stamped a little after five, so it hadn't been sitting unanswered on my phone for very long.

I typed out a quick text in reply.

Thanks for letting me know what happened. I don't think Det. Falco was annoyed with either one of us. Maybe with his deputies for not being thorough enough. But all's well that ends well, I suppose.

My finger touched the send button on the screen, and I dropped the phone back inside my purse, figuring I could continue the convo after I got home. I didn't want to delay any further, not with the two dogs and Edgar waiting for me at the house.

I'd only driven about a block before my phone binged again, telling me Malcolm must have replied. However, as much as I wanted to pull it out of my purse and take a look at what he had to say, I wasn't blessed with any convenient red lights where it would have been safe to do so and therefore had to wait until I reached my driveway and turned off the engine.

With any luck, the stone will be able to provide some evidence that's been missing. I was thinking about coming up to Salem tomorrow and seeing if you wanted to have dinner, but my department scheduled a last-minute meeting that I fear is going to run late, and I knew you would be busy as well, with it being Halloween. We'll just have to meet up on Saturday late afternoon. I thought I'd bring your costume by, and then we could go out for drinks before we head over to the dance.

Not exactly what I wanted to hear—I'd been hoping he might be able to bring my costume early, just so I'd have a chance to decide on an alternate if it turned out the one he brought from the drama department's collection was too skimpy—but I knew he was a busy person and would be booked up all day Friday. Otherwise, I might have risked driving down to Boston for an extended lunch, even though I knew All Saints Day was often as busy as Halloween itself, especially since this year a lot of people would be sticking around to attend the costume ball.

An answer possibly could have waited until I was inside the house, but I already had my phone out, and I figured an extra minute or so wouldn't be an issue.

Sounds good. I'm at 368 Winter Island Drive. What time were you thinking?

His response came back almost immediately, and I guessed he must have been watching his phone as well, possibly worried that I might take issue with the proposed schedule for Saturday.

I should be there around 5. That will give us

plenty of time to get changed and head out, since the doors to the ball don't open until 7.

Well, plenty of time for a guy. Since I didn't know what my costume would even be, I had no idea how much hair and makeup might be required for me to get ready.

But I figured I could do some basic evening makeup, and if it required anything more, I'd just pile that on top. I'd also need to close the store early, although I guessed people wouldn't have too much of a problem with that, not when so many of them would also be attending the ball.

That works. See you on Saturday!

See you then.

That exchange seemed to conclude the matter, so I dropped my phone back in my purse, undid my seatbelt, and made my way along the path that led to the front door. Once I opened it and stepped inside, though, I halted at once, not sure what to make of the scene in front of me.

Milo and Lexi stood off to one side, their expressions those of mirrored consternation, while Edgar had all of the rune stones laid out in the middle of the worn living room rug, and was even now frantically arranging and rearranging them as though he thought all he had to do was come up with the right configuration to make me understand what he was trying to say.

"I'm so glad you came home," Milo said. "Can you help him?"

Chapter 9

Alphabet Soup

I didn't know whether I could help Edgar or not. So far, I hadn't been of much assistance, other than giving him a neutral place to stay while he worked out his issues.

Gingerly, I closed the door behind me, although that didn't seem to disturb the raven at all. No, he just kept shoving the rune stones around with his beak, gaze fixed on the polished pieces of tiger's eye, and didn't even look up as I set my purse down on the little table near the entry.

"How long has he been doing this?" I asked.

Milo and Lexi looked at each other. In general, dogs weren't very good at estimating time, just because the way they experienced the world was so different from a human's perspective. But because Milo was a familiar, his canine brain wasn't quite the same as an ordinary dog's, and that was probably why he responded with, "Maybe an hour? I know I looked at the clock when he spilled all the stones out on the rug, and I think it was about half after four."

Well, at least Edgar hadn't been at this all day. Not for the first time, I wished I had a better way of communicating with Milo while I was at work; although I had a very basic cell phone that I left at the house while I was gone and which the dog could use to send me an emergency signal, it was supposed to be for times of utter urgency, like when the house was on fire or someone was trying to break in.

Clearly, Milo hadn't believed Edgar's sudden rune-stone spree was enough to merit a call like that, not when the dog knew it would send me rushing home in a panic.

"Do you have any idea what he's trying to say?" I asked, and Milo and Lexi both looked so perplexed that I wanted to laugh at their comical expressions.

However, none of this was a laughing matter.

"No," Milo replied, while Lexi nodded. "I don't understand those rune things at all."

That makes two of us, I thought. All right, that observation wasn't exactly the truth, since at least I'd read over the descriptions of the various runes and had a vague idea as to the concepts they were trying to convey.

Whereas even familiars, smart as they were, could have a tough time with the written word. I'd read that there had been witch companions in the past who'd been able to read spell books and had helped their mistresses that way, but I'd certainly never encountered one.

And if Milo couldn't even read plain old English, then I doubted he could figure out what the runes were saying...and what Edgar was trying to express with them.

Since he'd continued his obsessive arranging and rearranging of the stones the entire time the dogs and I had been speaking, it didn't seem as if he was paying too much attention to what was going on around him.

Time to see if the direct approach would work better.

"Edgar," I said, doing my best to make my tone firm but friendly at the same time. "Do you want to tell me what you're doing?"

To my relief, he looked up, gleaming dark eyes fixed on me. His wings spread, and he let out a fierce croak before pushing one of the stones with a taloned foot with such force that it rolled across the rug and smacked into my shoe.

Startled, I reached down and picked up the stone so I could inspect the angular markings carved into the tiger's eye. Which one was it? The Yew, which could symbolize strength, or the

Ansuz, which when reversed could mean betrayal and deception?

I'd left my laptop charging on the kitchen table, so I hurried in and grabbed it, then navigated to the rune lore website I'd bookmarked a couple of days earlier.

Yes, Ansuz. Betrayal, deceit.

But who was the deceiver, and who the deceived?

I had no idea. Was Eunice Bartlett the victim of someone who had deceived her...or had she been the betrayer, and been murdered in retaliation for her lies?

Once again, about a million questions, and no clear answers in sight.

I knew one thing, though. Whatever was going on, Edgar had become so agitated about it that he'd been desperately trying to find a way to drive his point home.

Gently, I closed the laptop lid and looked over at the raven. He was still pushing the stones around, but in a dejected way, as though he could tell that his frenzy of activity hadn't done him much good.

"It's okay, Edgar," I said. "I'll keep working on it. But now, I think we all need to have something to eat, okay?"

Both Milo and Lexi perked up at hearing those words—usually, I was putting food in their bowls almost the second I stepped inside the house—and even the raven seemed to realize he needed to get something in his stomach. He stepped away from the stones and surprised me by flapping his way from the rug to my shoulder.

Damn, he was a lot heavier than I'd thought he would be. I didn't exactly lose my balance, but I staggered for a second before I regained my footing and straightened. Luckily, he hadn't dug his talons into me.

"Okay, everyone," I said, doing my best to sound cheerful. "Chow time."

After dinner, Edgar didn't seem inclined to go back to messing around with the rune stones and instead curled up on his blanket, beak tucked under one wing. In a way, I was a little disappointed, since I'd been thinking that I needed to pull out his chunk of pyrite and see if I could find anything suspicious about it.

Not that I knew for sure whether it had anything to do with the chunk of stone the killer had used to attack Eunice Bartlett, but at least by inspecting Edgar's piece of fool's gold, I would have felt as though I was accomplishing something.

But instead, we all watched TV together, and I was in bed before ten. Just as well, I supposed;

although I wasn't opening the shop early or anything like that, tomorrow was Halloween, and I knew it would be more hectic than ever in downtown Salem. Doubly so, just because all the stores in our section of town were expected to have candy to hand out to any kids who visited during the day. And while I wouldn't waste time with an elaborate costume, I'd wear the black witch hat I usually reserved for formal coven meetings and a Victorian-inspired black dress I'd bought on Etsy a few years earlier, just so I wouldn't seem like a total party pooper.

Earlier, I'd decided it would be better for the animals to stay home; I couldn't have brought Edgar to the store, and it didn't seem fair to take the dogs with me and leave him at the house by himself. Lexi in particular had been disappointed, but I promised her some extra treats for being such a good dog, and that seemed to perk her up a bit, especially after I explained it had been so busy at the shop this week that she would have had to stay back in the stock room for most of the day.

All the same, she asked me if I could put on the witch costume I'd bought for her at the pet store, and Milo, sensing she wanted someone else to join in the Halloween fun with her, had offered to wear the black bandana printed with cheerful orange pumpkins around his neck as a way of showing holiday solidarity.

In a way, I was glad of the downtown festivities; my street was far too dark and had the houses spread too far apart for it to be considered a safe location for trick-or-treating, and this way I could get in the spirit of the season without having to bounce up and down like a jack-in-the-box every two minutes to answer the door and hand out candy.

When I crawled under the covers, though— and after Milo and Lexi took their usual places at the foot of the bed, and Edgar curled up in his blanket, which I'd set on the chair in the corner—I couldn't stop my thoughts from darting this way and that, trying to see if there was something in the puzzle of Eunice Bartlett's murder that I'd overlooked, some obvious piece of evidence that would point me straight to the killer.

Nothing presented itself, though, and eventually, my body made me go to sleep, as though realizing I wouldn't be of any use to anyone if I didn't get some rest.

And if I dreamed, I couldn't remember anything the next morning.

Not that I'd really expected to have prophetic dreams. Some witches might have had that gift, but I wasn't one of them. If I'd had some spare time to work with, I might have attempted a scrying. Unfortunately, what with making sure the animals were all fed and taking a little more care than usual with my hair and makeup that morning, I barely got out the door on time, especially since I also had to get Lexi and Milo in their Halloween costumes. Maybe no one else would get to see them, but I had to admit they were absolutely adorable, and grabbed a couple of quick pictures of them in their ensembles before I hurried out the door.

Traffic was wretched, and I swore under my breath as I inched toward my destination, praying all the while that no one had tried to steal my parking space. To my relief, the spot was open when I pulled in, and I grabbed my witch hat from its resting place on the passenger seat and hurried inside with only a minute to spare.

No sign of Sage, even though it was time to open up. However, she had even farther to drive than I did, and with the tourist traffic choking what felt like every damn street in Salem, I couldn't really be annoyed at her for not being on time.

Instead, I jammed my witch hat on my head, grabbed a couple of bags of candy from the stash in the stock room and poured them into a bowl, then trotted over to the cash register so I could grab the key and unlock the door.

Not a moment too soon, because people had already started to crowd the sidewalk outside. I greeted them with a smile and a "Happy Halloween"—and wondered how long it would take before I was utterly sick of the phrase.

Sage appeared a few minutes later, wearing a woodland nymph costume, all filmy and floaty in shades of green and brown, absolutely perfect for her coloring.

"Sorry I'm late," she said. "I haven't worn this thing for a year, and I couldn't find one of the damn shoes."

Which were delicate ballet flats with laces that went halfway up her calves, a perfect match to the costume. They weren't her usual style, though, which tended toward chunky Mary Janes when the weather permitted and boots when it didn't, so I could see why the costume's shoes might have ended up buried in the back of her closet.

"It's fine," I replied. "I barely made it on time myself. It'll be so nice when Halloween is over and we aren't fighting traffic every day to get to work."

"Seriously," she agreed. "If I wanted to do that, I would've moved to Boston."

I chuckled, but we didn't have time for much conversation after that, since more and more people packed into the store, some of them in costume, some of them wearing witch hats with street clothes, as though they thought that would be enough to pass for a Halloween costume. Seeing them, I was glad I'd put on my pretty dress, with its tight-buttoned bodice and full skirt, rather than opting for a pair of jeans and a themed sweater the way I had several times in the past when I just wasn't in the mood to do the full costume thing.

In fact, it seemed as though this year was busier than usual, which felt strange since Halloween hadn't even fallen on a Friday or Saturday. But maybe a lot of people had decided to turn the holiday into a four-day weekend, a theory only bolstered by the way there seemed to be far more kids roaming around than there normally would have been on a Thursday.

And after we got bombarded by a whole bus full of tweens from the middle school in neighboring Peabody, I realized that the bags of candy I'd laid away several weeks ago were never going to last until we closed at five-thirty.

"We're going to run out of candy," I told Sage as she passed me on the way to the cash register.

"Do you want me to run out and get some more?"

I hesitated. While it might have been better to have Sage handle the errand, I didn't want her to go out of pocket buying the candy. Yes, I could've pulled some money out of the register to fund the expedition, but that would have messed up my bookkeeping.

Better for me to do it.

"No, that's all right," I said, even as I performed a quick mental calculus to determine which store would be closest to my shop.

Probably the Market Basket. I'd just have to hope they weren't completely picked over. Yes, I was making the candy available as part of the greater downtown trick-or-treat event and not to kids on my street, but that didn't mean I wanted to hand out cellophane bags of candy corn or whatever.

"It should only take me about fifteen minutes," I went on, even as I hoped I wasn't being overly optimistic with that number. "You should be able to hang on that long, shouldn't you?"

"Sure," she replied with a grin that I thought was genuine. "Piece of cake."

I hoped she was right. The crowds didn't seem to have let up too much, although I had to admit the store felt a lot calmer without twenty middle-schoolers rampaging up and down the aisles.

"And you can go to lunch after I get back," I said. "It'll be almost noon at that point anyway."

She nodded—but also made a kind of shooing motion with one hand, signaling that I needed to get going and stop with the apologies.

I hurried out back, muttered a charm to keep my parking space open against my return, and then hopped into the Discovery, nearly mashing my tall witch hat in the process. After expelling an exasperated breath, I set the hat on the passenger seat and backed out, then pointed my SUV toward the closest grocery store.

While the traffic on the streets wasn't so great, I couldn't help being relieved when I pulled into the Market Basket's parking lot and saw that it was only about half full. Well, it might have been a special kind of holiday, but for most people, this Halloween was a regular workday, which meant they wouldn't be at the grocery store.

The candy section was a little picked over, but I was able to snag one of those big packs full of Kit Kats and Nestle's Crunch and various other goodies, and there was a lone bag of Snickers as well. I went to reach for it...

...only to have my hand nearly collide with one I knew all too well.

"N-noah?" I stammered, and took a step back.

He stood a few feet away, wearing his usual white lab coat over a button-down shirt and jeans. As far as I could tell, he seemed to have weathered our separation just fine—no dark circles under his eyes, no obvious weight loss. The same Noah Jenkins I remembered, six feet plus of gorgeousness, from the wavy brown hair I'd loved to run my fingers through all the way down to the tips of his loafer-clad toes.

No sign at all that he'd been pining away for me, which felt like even more of a punch in the gut.

"Hi, Charity," he said, sounding completely casual. Those piercing blue eyes surveyed me for a moment, taking in the witch hat—which I'd plopped on my head before walking into the store, figuring I might as well stay in the spirit—the black dress, the lace-up Victorian-style boots. Was that a flicker of amusement in his expression? He went on, "That's kind of on the nose, don't you think?"

"Wha—" I began, then realized he was talking about my witch getup. "Well, Halloween's easy when you can just pull stuff out of your closet, right?"

Maybe the barest nod. His gaze moved to the disputed bag of Snickers. "Were you going to buy that?"

"Not if you need it," I said quickly. "I can get that bag of Butterfingers instead. Stocking up for trick-or-treaters?"

"Something like that." His face now looked studiously neutral, as though he didn't want to give too much away. "Mrs. Muzzio informed me this morning that two bags of candy were never going to get me through Halloween in our neighborhood."

If anyone should know that, it would be the woman who lived across the street from his rented house. She'd lived there forever and seemed like a real busybody.

But I could see why they'd really need to stock up for Halloween on his street. It was lined with lovely Colonial-style and Craftsman homes that had been built in the late 1900s and early twentieth century, the kind of neighborhood where kids would feel safe to go out on their own if they were old enough. In fact, before our split, I'd sort of fantasized about what it would be like to be there with Noah handing out candy, since my own part of town really wasn't suited for that kind of activity.

Obviously, that particular fantasy wasn't going to come true.

"Well, I'm just getting stuff for the store, so you should definitely have the Snickers," I said.

A pause, and then he handed the bag over to me. "No, you can have it. I'll just get a few of these other ones."

Instinct made me take hold of the bag of Snickers, even as I wondered whether I should protest or just go with it. Since it seemed he'd only come here for candy and nothing else, he didn't have a shopping cart, just one of those plastic baskets meant to store a few quick items. He reached past me to pick up a bag of Twix and one of Milky Ways, along with some Mounds.

"Gotta get back to the clinic," he said, not meeting my eyes. "Have a happy Halloween."

"You, too," I responded. There, that had sounded almost natural...even though I doubted this Halloween would be very happy at all.

Despite that run-in with Noah, my trip to the Market Basket didn't take any longer than fifteen minutes, so I was back in time to let Sage go to lunch exactly as I'd promised. To my relief, the flow of customers eased a little while she was gone, probably because a lot of other people had gone off in search of their noonday meals as well.

I knew I sure wasn't hungry. Not after meeting Noah like that.

How dare he look so hale and hearty?

A lot of people probably would have argued that I was looking just fine on the surface as well, but I didn't want to admit that to myself. No, I'd needed to see some indication he was suffering, trying to figure out a way to reconcile despite his anger, and I hadn't noticed anything like that.

Unfortunately, he'd seemed just fine.

At least he hadn't mentioned having anyone else there with him at his house to hand out candy...not that that necessarily meant anything. Even if he'd already moved on, I kind of doubted he would have told me he had a hot date for Halloween. He might have still been angry with me, but he wasn't the sort of person to be cruel.

Sage came back a half hour later and told me she'd take over so I could get my own lunch. The idea still didn't seem very appealing, but I knew if I told her I wanted to skip lunch, she'd start trying to figure out why I'd suddenly lost my appetite.

That was why I went down the street to the sandwich shop, although I only got a bowl of minestrone soup and sat at the counter nursing it, knowing I should give myself this downtime even though I would much rather have been at the store getting distracted by assisting customers.

But I did get a text from Malcolm.

I hope you're having a good Halloween. Alicia told me she got your measurements, and she's hunting down costumes as we speak.

Well, that was something. I had to admit that at the moment, I wasn't feeling very Halloween-y, but at least I had the ball on Saturday night to look forward to. The day before, I'd dutifully sent off the necessary information to the wardrobe department head, and she'd responded that she would find something fun.

Since I didn't know the woman at all, I had no idea what her idea of "fun" was. I told myself I doubted she would have the date of a colleague wear something too daring, but you never knew.

I wouldn't express my doubts to Malcolm, though, not when I could tell he was doing his best to put together a fun evening for the two of us.

No, I did my best to compose a cheerful reply without being too chirpy.

That sounds great. It's busy at the store, so I'm glad I'll be able to go home and collapse afterward.

I suppose everyone is in Salem for Halloween.

Enjoy your quiet evening at home, and I'll see you on Saturday afternoon.

That seemed to signal the end of the conversation, so I just reacted to his text with a smiley face and left it there. If we'd been seriously dating, I might have used a heart emoji, but that seemed a bit much for a convo with someone I didn't know very well.

But at least our little back-and-forth helped to distract me a bit, and I finished the rest of my soup and headed back to the store.

The rest of the afternoon was just as hectic as the morning had been, although I was glad to see that our bolstered candy stash looked as though it was going to last through the end of the day. And really, the crowds started to taper off as we got closer to five, telling me that people were gearing up to go home and get into costume, or possibly get ready for their own set of trick-or-treaters.

Whatever the reason, the place emptied a few minutes before we were due to close, and I wondered whether I should lock up a little early so Sage and I could get the heck out of there. Because it was a weeknight, she was sticking close to home rather than heading down to Boston to party with her friends there, but I still guessed she'd be all too glad to have the chance to leave a bit before she'd expected to.

But then the shop door opened, and a man

walked in. He was tall, with medium brown hair and light brown eyes, maybe in his mid-twenties. No costume, just jeans and a dark green fleece pullover.

He caught sight of me behind the counter and headed straight over...even as I allowed myself a mental sigh at not being able to bail out early the way I'd been hoping.

"Can I help you?" I asked.

He was pleasant-looking rather than handsome, and something in the pallor of his face and the strain around his mouth told me he wasn't in here to just casually shop.

"Are you Charity Hughes?"

I nodded, although I didn't think my name mattered if he was here looking for some sort of cure.

"My name is Cade Bartlett," he said. "Eunice Bartlett was my mother."

Chapter 10

Sins of the Mother

An incongruous thought popped into my head as I stared at the man who'd just entered my shop.

You don't look old enough to be Eunice Bartlett's son.

True, I'd known she had a child, but because she'd been in her early sixties, I'd just assumed her son must be in his thirties somewhere. Women had children at a variety of ages, though, so I did my best to dispel the surprise I knew must have shown on my face and said, "I'm so sorry for your loss."

"It's okay," Cade Bartlett said quickly...more, I guessed, as a reflex than because he really thought it was all right. "I just wanted to come and see"—he swallowed—"see where it happened."

My heart ached for him. Sure, my mother and I had had our differences over the years, but I

157

couldn't begin to imagine what it would be like to lose her so suddenly, so violently.

"There isn't much to see," I said, but he only shook his head.

Sage had been over by the herb packets, tidying up what she could. It seemed she must have overheard my exchange with Cade Bartlett, because she came over to us, face incongruously solemn in contrast to the forest nymph costume she was wearing.

"I can show you," she said, voice full of sympathy. "I'm Sage—I'm the one who found your mother."

His gaze moved to her, and I thought I saw a flicker in his expression, as though he was surprised to see someone only a few years younger than he... and so pretty.

"Thanks," he replied. "I'd appreciate that."

"It's out back," she told him. "This way."

She led him away from the counter so they could go through the stock room and out to the parking lot and the spot where the dumpster was located.

I supposed it wasn't too surprising that Cade might have wanted to view the place where his mother had died—to make it seem real, I thought. Had he come here from the funeral home? The police department?

Hard to know for sure, and I wasn't going to

ask, not when he was so obviously in pain. Whenever a person died unexpectedly, there were always a hundred loose ends to be taken care of, so it seemed clear he'd come to Salem to handle whatever he needed to.

It was a lot for someone who looked to be only a couple of years out of college. Even though Malcolm had told me Eunice's son lived in Boston, he'd still had to drive an hour to get here, and I had no idea how many times he'd already gone back and forth from his hometown to the place where his mother had died.

He and Sage were outside for more than five minutes. I tried to get things tidied up as I waited, figuring I might as well do so now and have one chore out of the way when I returned to work the next morning.

Eventually, though, they came back inside. I couldn't say that Cade looked exactly happy, but something in his posture seemed a little less tense, and he even smiled as he thanked Sage and said he'd see her later.

After he left, I turned toward her, eyebrows questioning.

"'Later'?" I repeated.

She gazed back at me, deadpan. "He doesn't know anyone in Salem and I could tell he wanted to talk, so I said I'd meet him for dinner in a little while. I guess he was able to get a last-minute hotel room, but it wasn't ready when he checked in. That was why he came over here first. I didn't have any real plans for tonight except handing out candy at my mom's house, and I thought Cade needed a sympathetic ear way more than my mother needs help giving away chocolate bars."

Probably true. Then again, I remembered the admiring look in Cade's eyes as he caught sight of Sage for the first time, and I had a feeling this dinner of theirs wasn't just about having a sympathetic person to talk to about his mother.

He probably needed the distraction.

"That's nice of you," I told her. "I'm glad he won't feel so alone here in Salem. Dealing with tragedy is hard enough, but going through all that while the rest of the town is partying around you has got to be tough."

"Exactly," she replied. "Anyway, let's get locked up and get out of here, okay?"

A plan I definitely agreed with. I nodded, then got the keys so I could lock the front door. Sage went to the back and manned the light switches, and soon enough, we had everything closed up and ready to go for our next morning at the shop.

I told her I hoped she would have a nice dinner with Cade, then got into my SUV so I could drive home. Even though it was still fairly light out, I already saw groups of trick-or-treaters going from house to house in the neighborhoods I drove through, mostly the really little kids who couldn't stay out too late. Seeing them, I wondered whether I should have gone over to my mother's house, where she would have lots of Halloween visitors.

But no, that wouldn't have worked. Not that she wouldn't have loved to have me and the dogs, but taking care of Edgar put kind of a wrinkle on the situation. Most people weren't used to having a large raven hanging out in their living room.

Besides, the quiet evening ahead seemed the perfect time for me to break out the scrying mirror and see if I could use it to unearth any new information regarding Eunice Bartlett's death. After all, it was Halloween, All Souls, the night when the veil between the worlds was supposed to be at its thinnest, when spirits reached out from the afterlife to spin their tales of betrayal and woe...if you knew how to listen.

What better time to do my own exploration of someone's unexpected and tragic death?

Of course, the first order of business was to get all the animals fed this evening, with special treats that showed them I was honoring the holiday even if I had absolutely no intention of feeding them any chocolate. That meant chopped steak for the dogs, and a little more of the same for Edgar, mixed in with dried mealworms and some of the pellets Sally Hawkins had left for him.

He didn't seem nearly as agitated tonight. In fact, something about his behavior appeared almost resigned, as though he'd told himself he'd done his best, and if an obtuse human like me hadn't understood what he was trying to say, it wasn't on his shoulders.

No, it definitely wasn't his fault that I'd turned out to be so dense.

The three of them ate with a good appetite, and instead of reheating stew for the third day in a row, I indulged myself with a grilled cheese sandwich gloppy with muenster and jack and cheddar, accompanied by a glass of merlot.

After the day I'd had, I figured I'd earned it.

The animals seemed perfectly happy with sprawling in various spots in the living room while they digested their food after dinner, which meant I should have some undisturbed time to do my best to get to the bottom of Eunice Bartlett's murder. Down came the silver bowl from one of the cupboards, and out of the pantry came my big jug of moon water, which I'd prepared just the week before. I hadn't expected to need it any time soon, but these days, I did my best to make sure I always had some on hand.

A cloth already covered the kitchen table, so I set the silver bowl on top and carefully poured the moon water into it. No incantation at first, only the intention to keep my mind as open and receptive as possible, and to do my best to have the scrying be a true one.

But then it was time to get down to work.

By the shadows of the moon, dark secrets be unveiled,

Reveal the scene where blood has trailed,

Behind the dumpster, where silence screams,

Conjure the image from hidden dreams.

An image of the dumpster behind the building came into view for a few seconds, but then it shivered, became distorted, looking like something from the bad old days when your cable would go out and the screen would turn into something my mother and I often referred to as "baconvision."

And then the water in the silver bowl went completely black.

I stared down at it for a moment, hands on my hips. After getting home, I hadn't bothered to change out of my Victorian-inspired dress and boots, although I'd happily left the pointy witch hat on the table in the entry.

This was very odd. It wasn't as though I was the world's best scryer—far from it—but usually, if a particular seeing wasn't working, the water would stay blank the whole time. In this case, it seemed more as though the image had tried to form and then had been interrupted somehow.

Was there some kind of other magic blocking me? Had someone cast a spell to ensure that the events of that terrible night couldn't be spied on by another witch?

I really didn't like to entertain that idea, because then I'd also have to accept the ugly truth that it was a witch who'd killed Eunice Bartlett after all. My mother and I had already batted that idea back and forth, but we'd both decided it was a lot easier—and much less messy—to cast a spell of forgetting rather than engage in homicide.

Maybe that wasn't what was going on here at all. Although it looked as though something was blocking my spell, it could also be that I'd flubbed it somehow. I might not have been focused enough, could have been distracted.

Or possibly it was the energies of Halloween itself that were interfering with the enchantment. I'd never encountered anything like that before, but I also had to admit I wasn't always practicing magic on a night like this. When I was younger, the coven had always gathered on Samhain like clockwork, and yet as time had worn on, we'd found reasons to be busy elsewhere, and our practice wasn't nearly as regular as it once had been. People wanted to be out and socializing, or staying at home to hand out candy. And honestly, it had seemed smarter to engage in all the same activities as the mundanes so as not to attract attention.

Which meant I could be dealing with any number of factors here.

Well, no harm in trying again. If the image simply wouldn't come, maybe I'd break out my Tarot cards, even though I'd be the first to admit that I wasn't much of an expert in using them.

By shadowed alley, hidden deep,
Where whispers of the night do creep,
Behind the dumpster, blood runs cold,
Reveal the scene, the truth unfold.
In darkness veil, the crime laid bare,
Unmask the secrets, if you dare.

The water shivered again. For just the briefest moment, I caught an image of Eunice Bartlett in profile to me. Judging by the way her jaw was set and the way she angrily gestured with both hands, I thought she must have been arguing with someone, although the scrying mirror didn't reveal who it might have been.

And then the mirror went dark, and I knew deep down that it wasn't going to show me anything else that night.

Still, what I'd just witnessed felt like an important piece of the puzzle. Maybe I hadn't been able to see the person Eunice was talking to, but it seemed pretty clear she was having a heated discussion of some sort.

Heated enough to result in murder?

I had no idea. All the same, I filed the image

away in my mind, knowing that what I'd seen might be enough to explain why someone had decided to take her out of the equation, so to speak. Maybe six months ago, I wouldn't have been so ready to accept such an uncomfortable truth, but ever since Milo's mistress, Darla Fitzgerald, had been murdered back in May, I'd stumbled across enough murders to realize that more people than I might have wanted to acknowledge were capable of such a terrible thing.

The scrying mirror had done its job, so I took the bowl of moon water over to the sink and emptied it, murmuring a thank-you under my breath to the magically charged water for its help in getting me even that one brief vision. At the same time, I wondered what was going on with Sage and Cade, how their dinner had gone. She hadn't provided any real details about their plans, so I had no idea whether they had grabbed tacos at the Spitfire Grill or gotten an intimate table for two at Mercy Tavern.

Not that it was any of my business. The man had just lost his mother, and if he could find some comfort in talking to the stranger who'd discovered her body, I certainly wasn't going to begrudge him that.

Thinking of them at dinner at one of the places Noah and I had frequented still caused an inner pang, one that probably wouldn't have been so strong if I hadn't bumped into him at the Market Basket earlier today. Most of the time, our jobs and our schedules kept us in very separate orbits, but when they overlapped as they had today...

...well, it wasn't fun, that was for sure.

But I'd survived the encounter, and I told myself that as time went on, the hurt would grow less and less until at last, it was hardly anything more than a twinge.

Anyway, I had my date with Malcolm coming up on Saturday, and I knew I should be focusing on that. Deep down, I understood that our relationship couldn't go anywhere, not when he was bound and determined to prove witches were real and I was just as determined to make sure the world knew nothing about them, but that minor hitch wouldn't prevent me from having a little fun in the meantime.

With that thought to buoy me up, I placed the silver bowl on the countertop to dry, then blew out the white candles I'd lit to help cleanse the space. When I went out to the living room, I found Milo and Lexi sprawled across the couch, hind legs draped over each other, while Edgar seemed to sleep in his nest of threadbare blanket. I hated to wake them up, but I also knew they wouldn't like being left down here while I went to sleep.

So I roused them as gently as I could and gathered up Edgar's blanket, letting him ride on my shoulder as I mounted the stairs, while the two dogs brought up the rear. Soon enough, we were all bunked down for the night, although I found myself staring at the ceiling, my mind picking at the latest piece of evidence I'd seen.

Who had Eunice Bartlett been arguing with... and why?

To my relief, traffic was much better the next morning. Not improved all the way, since I knew a lot of people were staying over so they could attend the ball on Saturday night, but at least it seemed as if the casual Halloween day-trippers had gone home. In fact, I got to the store more than fifteen minutes early and put the time to good use making sure everything was in good order and we were ready to start the day.

Sage appeared about ten minutes after I'd started work, her expression cheerful.

"How was dinner?" I asked. Possibly I should have waited to broach the subject rather than pounce almost the minute she walked in the door, but it just seemed smarter to have this conversation before we were open to the public.

Her green eyes lit up with amusement. "It was fine. We went to Mercy Tavern—Cade had never been there, and the front desk people at his hotel were able to get us a table."

"This must all be very hard for him," I said.

At once, her expression sobered. "It is. His parents got divorced when he was really little and his dad kind of took off, from the sound of it, so he only ever had his mom for family."

I hadn't heard even a hint that Eunice had a husband who was active in her life, so this news didn't surprise me too much. "That's rough."

"It is," Sage replied. Her gaze flicked to the clock, as though gauging how much time we had left before the hordes descended. I didn't think we were going to be anywhere near as busy as we'd been the day before, but still, it was hard to have a private conversation with even three or four customers browsing our wares. "And he's feeling extra awful because he and his mom had a pretty bad fight a while back—I guess he's in the middle of getting his doctorate, and some of the stuff she pulled at the university, like arguing with the dean about putting some really questionable titles on her syllabus, put him in an awkward position."

"Didn't she resign?"

"Well, it sounds like she was mostly forced out, but her department tried to pass it off as early retirement. Anyway, Cade was living at home so he could save money while working on his dissertation, and I guess their fight was bad enough that he ended up moving out and sharing an apartment with a couple of other doctoral students."

None of that sounded very good. The image I'd seen in the scrying bowl the night before flashed into my mind—Eunice arguing about something, hands waving, expression a mixture of frustration and fury.

Had she been arguing with Cade?

Had he been so angry with what he saw as her antics that he'd snapped and bashed her on the head with that chunk of pyrite?

I didn't want to believe such a thing could be true, of course. Sure, I'd spent a total of five minutes around the guy, but he didn't feel like a killer to me.

Money could be a powerful motivator, though. And if he'd already been stressed, thanks to working on his dissertation, and then had the financial rug pulled out from under him, so to speak, maybe there was a chance he might have lost control and struck out at his mother.

Especially if there had been any kind of inheritance. Derek Falco hadn't mentioned anything like that to me, but I didn't see any reason why he should have. It sounded as though he'd talked to Cade on the phone and had viewed him as a grieving son and nothing more. As far as anyone knew, he hadn't even been in Salem on the night in question.

Not that that meant much. Boston was only an hour away, making it easy enough to come up here and commit mayhem if that was his plan.

"You're very quiet," Sage said then, and a gleam of suspicion entered her greenish eyes. They narrowed as she added, "You don't honestly think Cade had anything to do with his mother's murder, do you?"

"No," I replied, then amended, "I mean, I'm not sure. Some people might see Eunice Bartlett's actions at the university—actions that could have seriously affected her son's academic career—as motive enough to lash out in anger. And that doesn't even take into account whatever inheritance might be involved."

An emphatic shake of her head. "I only had dinner with the guy, but I can tell you he's not the type of person who could kill someone. He seems really upset about the whole thing. I guess the reason his mother came to Salem the other night was that she told him she had all the evidence she needed to prove her thesis about witches being real, and he just needed to be patient, that she'd be vindicated when she released it to the public."

This didn't sound good at all. I had to hope Dr. Bartlett had been overly confident and didn't actually have much that would prove the truth about witches to the world. The last thing we needed was a repeat of the incident with Darla

Fitzgerald, who had almost betrayed us all when she discovered her long-lost twin brother, a man whose own deadly powers and overwhelming rage had proved to be her undoing. Darla and Brad Alatorre had plotted to release videos taken at the Witch Olympics to show that witches truly did exist, but through a lot of bumbling luck—and with Milo's help—I'd been able to stop Darla's murderous brother.

The Witch Olympics committee had sworn that all those tapes had been destroyed, and since they'd done so while operating under a truth spell, the magical community had taken their word for it. I didn't think that was what we were dealing with here, but since our secrecy depended on each of us doing her very best to conceal our magic, I could see why a single slip-up, accompanied by the timely use of a cell phone camera, might have been enough to give Eunice Bartlett the evidence she needed.

But if she'd truly caught something on video, why the last-minute trip to Salem...and to the little block of shops that contained my store...a trip that would ultimately prove fatal to her?

Once again, I didn't have a single satisfactory answer.

"Cade didn't say what that evidence was?" I asked, and Sage shook her head.

"No. I don't think he knew, either. It sounded

like it was some sort of surprise that his mother wanted to reveal to him when she was ready."

A revelation that had never taken place. But while I supposed Cade Bartlett could be a consummate liar, my instincts were telling me he was innocent, a man pulled into a tragedy that was none of his doing.

When I didn't reply right away, Sage went on, "It sounds like he's going to be here for a couple of days, since there's a lot he has to deal with. We plan to meet for dinner again tonight. He's pretty much on his own, and I wanted to be there to help him out if I could."

I had a small notion of all the various matters he would have to handle in the wake of his mother's death, just because my mom and I had had to do a lot of that very same thing some five years ago when my grandmother died. In her case, it had been a fatal heart attack in her sleep and not an unprovoked murder, but still, death always involved a lot of paperwork. Cade could probably use a sympathetic ear.

"That's nice of you," I said, and her shoulders lifted.

"I'm just glad I could be around and make sure he wasn't having to do everything all on his own."

There were several more questions I wanted to ask, but it was nearly ten and time to unlock the door and get business started for the day. And although I guessed that Sage probably would have answered those questions, I also got the impression she was glad of the arrival of that morning's patrons so she wouldn't be pressed for any more information regarding Cade Bartlett.

That was all right. I had my own ways of digging up any bits of data I might need.

Chapter 11

Scrabbling for Clues

Derek, unfortunately, wasn't all that forthcoming when I called him on my lunch break. I'd been hoping that, since he'd kept me so up to date on what had happened with the medical examiner's findings, he'd also be just fine with giving me a little more background on Cade Bartlett. I still didn't think Eunice's son was the culprit, but I also got the impression that Sage liked him a lot, and I knew I'd feel awful if I hadn't done my best to prevent her from developing a relationship with someone who wasn't quite as squeaky-clean as he appeared at first glance.

"I can't really talk about the particulars," Derek told me over the phone as I sat in the back booth at the sandwich shop and nibbled at my roast beef on sourdough. The day before, I wouldn't have been able to get such a good seat, but the crowds had thinned out considerably today. "All I can say is that we looked into Cade Bartlett and didn't find anything that merited further investigation."

"So, he has an alibi for his whereabouts the night of his mother's murder?"

A small chuckle came through my phone's speaker. "Trying to solve this one for me, Charity?"

"No," I said hastily, even though that was pretty much exactly what I was doing. "I guess I'm just trying to put the pieces together. My assistant Sage talked to him, and it sounds like she's sort of being a shoulder to lean on while he's here in Salem. I guess I just want to make sure she's not getting herself into anything dangerous."

Derek didn't answer right away, as though he was deciding how much he would allow himself to say to alleviate my worries...while at the same time not revealing anything truly important. But then he said, "He has an alibi—a good one. There's no way he could have been in Salem the night of the murder."

Well, that was something. All the same, I wished Derek had told me exactly what Cade's alibi was. If he'd been teaching a class in front of dozens of watching eyes, that was one thing. But if he'd had a friend vouch for him...that was an entirely different circumstance, as far as I was concerned.

Unfortunately, I could tell from the firmness in

Derek's tone that he wasn't going to let me push things too much further.

"So I don't think you need to worry on behalf of your assistant," he went on. "Cade is grieving, but he's been cooperative. For now, all I can do is keep on doing what I've already done—interview colleagues and friends, and try to see if there's anyone in Dr. Bartlett's world who would have wanted to cause her harm. So far, I haven't found much, but we're in the early stages of the investigation."

He stopped there, and once again, I could tell he wasn't going to volunteer anything more than what he'd already told me.

"Thanks, Derek," I said, hoping I sounded sincere. "That is something of a relief. I'll let you get back to work."

"It's not a problem," he replied. "It's logical that you would want to make sure that your assistant wasn't putting herself in any danger."

We ended the call there, and I put my phone back in my purse so I could finish eating that delectable roast beef sandwich. All the same, I couldn't help feeling just a wee bit dissatisfied.

Something was going on here...but I didn't seem to have the luck or the skill to figure out what it was.

The rest of the afternoon moved faster than I'd thought it would, though, maybe because we were still busy enough that I didn't have a lot of time to brood over my failings as an amateur detective. Sage seemed relieved that I hadn't kept pressing her on the subject of Cade Bartlett, but really, what else was there to say? The police didn't think he was a suspect, which meant I shouldn't be looking at him that way, either.

Even if I couldn't quite help myself, mostly because I didn't have any other prospects.

But my goodbye to her at the end of the day sounded natural enough, and honestly, I was glad she'd found someone to connect with, even if the reason for their meeting had been a tragic one.

At least she wasn't going home to an empty house.

Oh, stop it, I scolded myself as I backed out of my parking space and began maneuvering into the traffic on Broad Street. *I'll bet if you'd given Derek even the slightest hint that you were interested, you wouldn't be sitting home alone tonight.*

Maybe so. Not for the first time, I wondered why I kept holding Derek Falco at arm's length when I'd seemingly had no problem accepting Malcolm Grimes' invitation to the Halloween ball.

The answer was pretty simple, actually. Even if I was ready to move on from Noah...and that was a pretty big "if"...dating someone local like Derek presented a lot more problems. If things didn't work out, then that would mean there would be two people here in town I'd have to work hard to avoid.

Whereas if all Malcolm and I had was a single date at the Halloween dance, what difference would it make? He lived in Boston and I lived in Salem, and it would be extremely easy to never see each other again after Saturday night.

It occurred to me that, while I'd been interested in investigating Cade, I hadn't put much effort into finding out more about Malcolm Grimes. Pretty much all I knew was that he taught history at Roxbury University...and that he was determined to prove witches were just as real as doctors and lawyers.

Looked like I'd figured out what to do with myself on this particular Friday night.

First, of course, was greeting the animals and petting Milo and Lexi, and then getting all our dinners ready. Just as I'd been doing for the past few days, I took my bowl of reheated stew out to the living room—thank God this was the last of it —and settled myself on the couch. Edgar and the dogs wolfed down their food soon enough and came out to join me.

"How was everything here?" I asked, and Milo's tail thumped against the floor.

"Fine," he replied. "Quiet."

"Edgar didn't do much of anything," Lexi chimed in. "He didn't even touch those rune stones."

I looked over at the raven, who'd settled himself on his blanket. He looked healthy and hale enough, plumage still shiny and lying smoothly against his body, brown eyes bright. Even so, it felt to me as though something about him was drooping, as if he'd given up on trying to communicate with anyone and had resigned himself to hanging out here until I decided he was an impossible case and sent him back to his mistress.

That wasn't going to happen any time soon. I generally kept familiars for a week, sometimes even more, depending on what needed to be done, and since Edgar had only been here for a couple of days, I still had time to figure this out.

Although I had absolutely no idea how.

"Maybe he was tired," I said, and took a bite of stew.

The two dogs exchanged a glance. I could tell they didn't think Edgar had any reason to be tired, not when he didn't do anything except sit around the house all day.

But it also seemed they didn't want to protest, not with him sitting a few feet away and listening to everything we said.

"How was the shop?" Milo asked politely, and

I had to keep myself from smiling at the sudden change of subject.

"It was fine," I said. "Busy, but not too bad. And just one more day until we'll all have some time together."

He nodded, and Lexi looked relieved. Her former master had taken her to work with him, but I had decided against doing the same thing, not when it wasn't really feasible to bring Milo as well. It seemed better to me for the two of them to stay home where they could entertain each other—and go out into the yard through the doggy door as needed. Things were a little different with Edgar here, but still, I hadn't changed their routine very much.

But both dogs always looked forward to Sundays and Mondays, when I'd be home almost the entire time unless I had errands I needed to run. And honestly, after the week I'd had, I was glad my days off were rapidly approaching.

First, though, I had to get through Saturday at the store...and the dance that followed.

"Want me to turn on *Animal Planet?*" I asked as I set down my empty bowl. "You can watch TV while I look some stuff up on my laptop."

Both dogs nodded, and Edgar stretched out his neck, which I hoped was his way of signaling that he was also fine with me having the TV going in the background.

So I picked up the remote and turned on the television, then got my bowl and took it into the kitchen. A quick rinse, and I put it in the dishwasher before heading over to the spare room I used as an office. At least I'd had the presence of mind to plug my laptop into its charger after the last time I'd used it, so it was ready to go.

Everyone had hunkered down in their favorite TV-watching spot in the living room, and I sat down on the couch and opened up the computer. From there, it wasn't too hard to navigate to Roxbury University's website so I could get the official skinny on Malcolm Grimes.

What I found there was pretty much what I had expected—a brief bio stating how long he had been tenured there, and a list of his publications, which was impressively lengthy, considering he was only forty-two years old. With all those books and papers, how had he found the time to teach classes, too?

Well, his schedule wasn't really any of my business. No, what I needed wasn't anything I could find on the university's website.

Some quick Googling pulled up a few more tidbits—he'd been married and divorced, with no children. Like me, he was an only child.

Unlike me, though, his family had money. A lot of money, from what I could tell, an inheritance that had come to him a few years earlier when his father passed away. His mother had died in a car accident when he was just in high school.

That must have been a terrible ordeal to suffer at such a young age, but the articles I'd found didn't go into any huge detail, which didn't surprise me too much. It wasn't as if his therapist would have volunteered to give away all his secrets.

I supposed I was a little surprised that Malcolm was so involved in his university career when it looked as though he didn't have to work at all. More than once, I'd wondered if I would keep the store going if I didn't need that income to maintain my lifestyle. If a prosperity spell had gone a little overboard and gotten me a Powerball windfall, would I still go to Full Moon Apothecary every day and deal with a demanding and sometimes down-right obnoxious public?

To be honest, probably not. Sure, I would always keep on making my potions and elixirs because I knew they helped people, but there were other ways of getting those cures into clients' hands without maintaining a storefront.

It seemed to me that Malcolm Grimes felt he had a calling...a calling that included trying to prove witches were real.

I closed the laptop and stared forward, but I wasn't paying any attention to the nature documentary currently showing on the TV. No, I could feel myself frowning, trying to figure out why someone like Malcolm Grimes—rich, attractive, successful—would have any interest in dating a woman as outwardly ordinary as I was. I had to believe there were probably dozens of prospects in Boston who would have been thrilled to attend the Halloween ball with him.

And yet he had asked me.

One of those mysteries of the universe to be puzzled out at a later date. After all, Derek seemed interested in me, and Noah and I had shared a wonderful relationship until he decided he couldn't handle the secrets I'd been compelled to hide, so it wasn't as though I'd never attracted handsome men.

But still, on the surface, Malcolm and I seemed like an odd couple, just because of the age difference if nothing else.

Maybe he had a thing for redheads.

Since he hadn't texted me to cancel our date—and had sent a brief note toward the end of the afternoon saying that he was looking forward to seeing me the next day—it didn't seem as though he was having second thoughts about our date for the Halloween ball.

And because it didn't feel as if he was going to change his mind in the time remaining, I knew I'd just have to roll with it and see what happened.

If only I could get that awkward encounter with Noah at the Market Basket out of my thoughts...and if only I could ignore the niggling feeling in the back of my mind that this date with Malcolm was still cheating despite having been broken up for more than a month.

Sometimes, my brain could be extremely irritating.

To distract myself, I put the laptop on the coffee table and then reached for Edgar's pouch of rune stones, only a few inches away from the spot where I'd set my computer. The stones had been sitting there for more than a day now, and it seemed I really should be trying to do more with them. And since Halloween had come and gone, I didn't have the excuse of being too tired and over-worked any longer.

Edgar sat up in his blanket nest, bright eyes watching me closely.

"Do you want to try this again?" I asked him, and he immediately hopped over to me, landing on the side of the coffee table that wasn't occupied by my laptop.

I tried not to wince. Yes, the table already had its fair share of scratches and wear marks, but....

The coffee table wasn't important, though. The important thing was what I could get the raven to tell me.

After loosening the ties on the little velvet pouch, I shook the carved tiger's-eye stones onto the tabletop. Edgar watched me, eyes keen and sharp.

"I want to understand," I told him. "But you have to be patient with me, because I'm new to using these things and have to look everything up. Is that okay?"

In response, he reached out with his beak and pushed a single stone toward me, one marked with a simple "X." I picked up my laptop and opened the lid, then went to the website I'd bookmarked a couple of days earlier.

"*Gebo*," meaning "gift." It was a positive rune, one that could mean several different things. One of them, though, was generosity, and I thought I had an idea of what Edgar was trying to express.

"Is this your way of saying thank you?" I asked, and he dipped his head, pushing the stone a little closer to me.

That sure looked like a "yes" to me, and a pang of guilt knotted my stomach.

"I haven't done very much," I said, knowing how doubtful I sounded, but Edgar, apparently undeterred, let out a harsh croak, as if to tell me he knew I was doing my best.

Or this could all be coming from my imagination, and in reality, I still had absolutely no idea what the raven was trying to communicate.

But since I knew I needed to take a stab at this —or I might as well give up and ask Sally to come and get her familiar—I told myself I needed to be a little more confident in my ability to puzzle out what the raven was saying. It would have been a lot easier if he'd decided to start communicating with Scrabble tiles, but since we were stuck with runes, I had to do what I could.

"Do you know why you started talking with the runes?" I asked.

At once, he shuffled through the scatter of stones before pushing one toward me, a symbol I'd already begun to recognize. The flag-like symbol, *Ansuz*, or message.

But the reverse of its meaning was deception, and I guessed that was what Edgar was trying to convey now.

"Someone deceived you?"

He ruffled his feathers, then knocked his beak against the tabletop, creating a fresh scar.

Well, I'd been thinking about getting a new coffee table for a while now.

"Someone is using you as a means for their deception?"

He croaked again, which I thought might have been his way of saying yes.

"Who?" I asked, then realized it wasn't the sort of question that either the runes or a simple yes-or-no exchange would be able to answer. "Someone you know?"

Another of those raspy "caws," so much deeper

and throatier than the sound an ordinary crow would make.

Suspicion began to grow. Not the sort of thing I wanted to believe, but since Milo had come to me because of a spell his mistress had placed on him, I knew this sort of situation wasn't what you could call unprecedented.

"Was it Sally?"

Edgar croaked again, wings beating in agitation, so violently that Milo got to his feet and started to come over to us, clearly ready to protect me if the raven didn't calm down.

"It's fine, Milo," I said quickly. Lexi had also gotten up, but because Edgar seriously outmatched her, she'd kept a safe distance. "We're just trying to get something figured out."

Milo made a low, growling sound in his throat, and I stared at him, surprised. He was a gentle dog and not the type to be aggressive at all, but I could tell he thought our raven guest had stepped way over the line.

To my relief, Edgar folded his wings against himself, but his head kept bobbing up and down, over and over again, as if he needed to make sure I understood his response.

Although I couldn't cuddle him the way I might have an upset Lexi or Milo, I still reached over and ran my hand down his neck and along his back, hoping the slow, soothing motion might help him to calm down a little more. He relaxed against my fingers, giving weight, and I knew he'd received the message.

While I was outwardly calm, my thoughts wouldn't stop racing.

Sally was using him to deceive someone? But who...and why?

My gaze slid toward the clock on the mantel. Only a little past eight-thirty, which meant it wasn't too late to contact Sally Hawkins and see if I could get to the bottom of Edgar's latest communication with me.

Now I just had to work up the nerve to do it.

Chapter 12

Boom or Busted

"Oh, I think Edgar misunderstood the situation," Sally Hawkins said, giving a little laugh that was almost but not quite a giggle.

I cocked an eye at the entrance to my office, but it seemed Milo and Lexi and Edgar had understood I wanted some privacy and had remained in the living room with the television on.

Even as I'd worked up the nerve to contact Sally, I'd decided I would rather make the call from my office, where I wouldn't have the animals listening in and where I could close the door if necessary. Although Edgar had seemed pretty adamant, I knew the rune stones weren't the most precise form of communication out there, and I wanted to get his mistress's side of the story.

"So...what *is* the situation?"

"I've started seeing someone," she told me. "A mundane, obviously. He wanted me to go with him to Cape Cod for a few days, and I couldn't think of what to do with Edgar except to have him go stay with you. It's not as if you can drop a raven off at the local dog boarding facility."

No, you couldn't. Not that I'd ever heard of a witch leaving a more traditional familiar—whether dog, cat, or rabbit—with a pet sitter. They were supposed to be inseparable, although I supposed in case of an emergency, a witch could get someone from her coven to watch the animal if necessary.

"So, you're in Cape Cod now?" I asked, since that was the first thing that popped into my mind. Annoyance had already flared at the way she'd used me as her pet-sitting service, but biting her head off wouldn't do anything to fix the situation.

"Yes," she replied. "Hank's in the shower right now, or I probably would have let this go to voicemail."

I supposed it would be kind of hard to explain away a conversation about your raven familiar. And I'd have to be the last person to condemn Sally for keeping her witchy nature secret from her new boyfriend, considering how I'd done that same thing to Noah and had been just fine with keeping him in the dark.

Until fate forced my hand, of course.

"Did you put a spell on Edgar to make him talk

in runes?" I asked next, and Sally gave a nervous laugh.

"I suppose it was kind of a silly spell," she said. "But I had to think of something harmless but which would still give me a reason to have him stay with you for a while. Obviously, I'll remove it once I get back."

I tried not to sound judge-y, but I wasn't sure whether I was entirely successful. "And when will that be?"

"Monday," she replied at once. "I should be home by early afternoon. Maybe I can come get Edgar on your lunch break?"

"Oh, the shop's closed on Mondays," I told her. "Usually, I run errands on my days off, but I can arrange to be home at a time that works for you."

"Well, I can be pretty flexible," she said at once. "Like I said, I should be back sometime on Monday afternoon, so you can call me then."

"I'll let you know when I'll be around," I told her. "I'm just glad to hear this was a misunderstanding and nothing more."

Another of those nervous not-quite giggles. "Oh, I'm sure Edgar wanted to be dramatic about it. He doesn't really approve of Hank. But he's a nice man, and I know Edgar is only being jealous because he's had me to himself all these years."

I supposed I could see that happening. My situation with Milo was very different, partly because he wasn't exactly my familiar but rather a beloved member of the family, and partly because he'd adored Noah from almost the moment he set eyes on him.

That was the last thing I wanted to think about, though. My lies and deception—even if they'd been necessary—had taken away the man both Lexi and Milo absolutely loved. Neither of them had said anything about the cause of the breakup to me, probably because Milo would have explained to Lexi why it was important for witches to keep their magic a secret, and yet I knew they missed him almost as much as I did.

I wondered what Sally would do if she decided to make things permanent with Hank. Tell him the truth, I supposed, since witches had been doing that very thing for centuries...once they were sure their partner was the person they'd be with for the rest of their lives. However, that wouldn't solve the problem with Edgar. About all I could do was hope the raven would become reconciled to the situation as time wore on.

Whatever ended up happening, it really wasn't my problem. Much more important was that Sally had cleared up the mystery of why Edgar was so fond of the deception rune, and that it sounded as if she would come to fetch her raven sometime on Monday.

Yes, one mystery might have been solved...but I still had a much bigger one to occupy my thoughts.

———

Edgar hadn't seemed very satisfied when I told him I'd worked things out with Sally, but I supposed his attitude could have been him sulking over the realization that she wasn't about to give up her boyfriend just because her familiar wasn't on board with the relationship. However, he hadn't gone back to the runes to try to press his side of the story, which seemed to me an admission that he knew he'd been in the wrong—or at least, wasn't entirely in the right.

And I slept better than I'd thought I would, and bounced out of bed the next morning with a lot more energy than I might have expected, given how busy the previous week had been.

But it was Saturday, and I'd be going to the Halloween ball tonight.

First up, though, was a full day at work.

Again, I got there early, mostly because there wasn't any traffic to speak of and I sailed right into my parking space at the back of the store with hardly a hiccup. I chose to take that as a sign that the rest of my day would go smoothly, and realized I was smiling as I unlocked the back door and went inside to disarm the alarm.

A bit of tidying up, and then Sage arrived as well, wearing a smile that appeared to be a mirror of my own.

"Hey," she said as she came out to meet me at the cash register.

"Hey," I replied. "One more day, and then I think we'll be pretty much back to normal."

"Or all the way there, if the drive to work was any indication."

I thought she was probably right. Sure, we still had plenty of people staying over for the Halloween dance, but since the tourists didn't have to compete with Salem's regular commuters on this Saturday morning, today felt like any other regular day.

"How is Cade doing?" I asked, and she lifted an eyebrow.

"He's okay," she said. "It's hard for him because he doesn't have any other family to speak of. I guess his mother's cousin is driving here to help him make the arrangements to get her back to Boston, since the coroner...." Sage stopped there, obviously not wanting to say something as blunt as, *The coroner released the body.* She pulled in a breath, then continued. "Anyway, they need to get Dr. Bartlett back to Boston. And then he'll be heading back, too, since he T.A.'s a class on Monday morning."

Pretty sad that the university wouldn't allow

him some bereavement leave, but maybe this had been his choice. I knew a lot of people who would much rather keep powering through than allow themselves a chance to pause and breathe.

Sage's expression was almost too neutral, and I got the feeling she was doing her best to hide her emotions because she didn't want to show that she'd realized she would miss him. The entire two years she'd been working for me, she'd never had a serious boyfriend and instead preferred to go out with groups of friends when socializing. I didn't know for sure whether that was because she wasn't ready for any kind of commitment...or whether she simply wasn't willing to enter into a relationship where she might at some point have to admit the truth about the witchy world to him.

But it seemed she liked Cade a good deal more than she'd planned to. Boston was only an hour away, though, so it wasn't as if they couldn't continue the connection once he was past the fallout from his mother's death and ready to have some kind of a personal life again.

Well, that was all far off in the future...if it happened at all.

For now, it was enough to get the shop opened and to greet that morning's customers—and to cast a wary eye at the sky, since it was starting to get cloudy. The Halloween ball was being held indoors, true, but that didn't mean any of the people attending would be thrilled to drag their costumed selves from the parking lot to the venue in the rain.

By moonlight's grace, the skies stay clear,
No raindrops fall, no rain comes near.
With starlit charm, protect this night,
Costume ball shines in dry delight.

Usually, I didn't interfere with the weather, but I wasn't doing anything too extreme, was only asking for any rain to hold off until tomorrow morning. The clouds could stay; in fact, they would probably help contribute to the spooky atmosphere at the dance, so there was no reason to make the charm any stronger than it was.

We had steady streams of shoppers that morning, not enough to make it too crazy, only just right. Sage and I answered questions and rang up sales, and the skies outside remained cloudy but dry, telling me my spell was doing its job. In fact, as the day wore on and was utterly unremarkable in every way, I chose to take that as a sign that my evening would unspool in much the same fashion. Malcolm and I would go to the party, have a drink or two, maybe dance...although I had to admit I had a difficult time visualizing that part of the evening...and then we'd realize we had absolutely zero chemistry and could both go on with our lives.

The problem with signs, though, was that they could change on a dime.

Around two o'clock, at least four squad cars and SUVs pulled up in front of Curious Collections, an antique shop across the street and a few stores down the block. Those of us in the witch community tended to steer clear of the place, mostly because its owner, Trent Abernathy, had what we viewed as an unhealthy interest in the occult, and we didn't want to say or do anything that might attract his attention.

However, just because he included antique Ouija boards and preserved skulls he claimed were from Nigerian witch doctors among the eclectic offerings in his shop, I couldn't think of what Trent could have possibly done that would have required that kind of police presence at his business.

Everything in my store came to a halt as Sage and I and the half dozen or so customers who'd been browsing our wares crowded around the front window, peering out so we could get a good view of the goings-on across the street. The police officers swarmed the entrance to Curious Collections, guns drawn, and then proceeded inside, with Derek Falco bringing up the rear.

What in the world was going on?

We couldn't see what was happening inside the store, but a couple of startled shoppers emerged a minute later, fleeing in either direction down the sidewalk, and then a short time after that, the deputies emerged, escorting a handcuffed Trent Abernathy.

They took him over to one of the squad SUVs and put him in the back seat, and then they all went to their respective vehicles. Derek was the last to leave; it looked to me as though he must have acquired Trent's shop keys, because he locked the door behind him before getting in his unmarked police sedan and driving off.

Sage turned and looked at me, wide-eyed, while my customers murmured amongst themselves.

"Party's over," I announced cheerily. "Let's get back to shopping, shall we?"

The shoppers moved away from the window, still obviously discussing what they'd just witnessed. I couldn't really blame them for being shocked—it wasn't as if we had the equivalent of a SWAT raid on bustling, cheerful Essex Street every day.

To be honest, I couldn't remember ever seeing something like that go down before. It wasn't as if there was no crime in Salem, but most of the time, all our police department had to deal with was residential or commercial burglaries, or maybe the rare domestic violence call.

My fingers itched to pick up the phone and call Derek to find out what the hell was going on, but I had a feeling he must be pretty busy right around now.

Well, I'd just have to wait.

———

To my surprise, he was the one who reached out first. About two hours later, just as things were winding down and Sage and I were getting ready to close the store early so I could go home and get ready for the Halloween ball, my phone rang.

"I suppose you saw what happened at Curious Collections earlier this afternoon," came Derek's voice, and I made a face that was halfway between a grimace and a smile.

Luckily, he couldn't see me. "Well, considering we had almost a front-row seat...yes, we saw it."

Along with several tourists who'd looked uncertain as they paid for their purchases, as though they were thinking they weren't sure they planned to make a return visit to Salem any time soon. I hoped they wouldn't allow that one extremely isolated incident to color their opinions of my hometown. Usually, it was just as quaint and picturesque as all the pictures and postcards showed...as long as you stuck to the more historic sections of town...but I also couldn't pretend it was all sunshine and roses.

"I think we can consider the Bartlett case closed," Derek went on, and I blinked.

"What do you mean?"

"I mean we got an anonymous tip that Trent Abernathy was the person who'd murdered Eunice Bartlett, so we followed up...and found a piece of pyrite in his store that was big enough to have been the murder weapon. It also had a chunk missing. Right now we're analyzing it against the pyrite fragment you and Malcolm Grimes found under the dumpster, but I have every reason to believe it's a match."

For a moment, I just stood there, cell phone still pressed to my ear, as I tried to process what Derek had just told me.

Why in the world would Trent Abernathy murder Eunice Bartlett?

Who knew? But it sure seemed Derek was convinced of his guilt, and I had to admit that the owner of Curious Collections had always given me an icky vibe. Maybe Eunice had come into possession of a relic Trent coveted, and when she wouldn't sell it for what seemed like a fair price, maybe he'd stalked her and then bashed her over the head so he could take it for his own.

Of course, that begged the question of why he'd be stupid enough to take the murder weapon back to his store, but I supposed he might have thought the best thing to do was hide it in plain sight. His store was so full of miscellaneous junk that I could see why he might have believed he'd be able to get away with displaying it amongst the rest of his "treasures."

I found my voice and asked, "Has he said why he would do such a terrible thing?"

"No, he claims he's innocent. He won't say anything other than that—he's trying to find an attorney."

Good luck with that at four o'clock on a Friday afternoon. I supposed he could reach out to a criminal defense lawyer in Boston, where there would be a much larger pool of attorneys to draw from, but until his counsel was set, it sure sounded as though Derek wasn't going to get a whole lot more out of Trent.

"That's...that's great news," I said, since I didn't know how else I should respond. Derek sounded confident, even upbeat, but a niggling little worry surfaced in my brain despite his apparent belief that this was an open-and-shut case.

What if Trent wasn't the killer? What if someone had set him up?

I had no idea why anyone would do that, but maybe it wasn't personal. It seemed possible to me that the real killer had decided he was the most likely suspect and had planted the evidence somehow.

Honestly, there wasn't a lot of "somehow" about how they might have managed to do such a thing.

Since I'd been in his store once or twice, I knew Trent didn't have any kind of real security system. The truly valuable stuff was tucked away in locked cases, but otherwise, someone could have come in with the pyrite hidden in a backpack or purse and then set it down somewhere when he wasn't looking.

Or I could be grasping at straws because the current story didn't seem to fit my preconceived notion of how the case should be solved.

In other words, by me.

"Yes, it's always good when we can get to the culprit quickly," Derek said. "And we'll let a jury of his peers decide if his claims of innocence are warranted. For now, though, Abernathy is locked up, and I doubt the judge is going to allow bail because of his priors."

"'Priors'?" I echoed, genuinely startled.

Derek chuckled. "Not murder. He got a suspended sentence over a battery case eight years ago, but because the charge involved physical violence, I'm pretty sure the judge will think it more believable that Abernathy might have graduated to murder if the stakes were high enough." He paused, then said, "Anyway, I just wanted to let you know about the latest developments. It looks like we can all breathe a sigh of relief now."

"Sure does," I murmured, doing my best to ignore an uneasy feeling in my stomach, one that didn't quite want to go away. "Thanks for the update."

He told me it was nothing, and we ended the call there.

I slid my phone into my purse, which I'd already set down under the counter in preparation to lock things up for the day.

"Was that about Trent Abernathy?" Sage asked. She'd been standing close enough to have overheard the whole conversation, although I doubted she'd been able to pick up on everything Derek had said.

"Yes," I replied. Because I hadn't been given any of that information in confidence, I figured it was safe enough to fill her in. "It sounds like the police found incriminating evidence in Curious Collections that's directly connected to Eunice Bartlett's murder, so Derek's pretty sure they caught their killer."

My assistant's expression was a mixture of relief and consternation. "I can't believe we've had a killer running the store across the street for all those years."

"Suspected killer," I said, although I decided not to mention that I wasn't entirely sure the Salem police had the right person. "But it doesn't sound like Trent's going to get bail, so at least he'll be locked up until the trial."

Whenever that was. Several months at least, I

guessed, but I had to admit I was kind of hazy on the timeline for those sorts of things.

"That'll be such a relief for Cade," Sage replied. "I know he hated the idea of the person responsible for his mother's death still being out there somewhere."

I hadn't much liked it, either. And I supposed it was possible those nervous quivers in my stomach had everything to do with my upcoming date with Malcolm Grimes and nothing at all regarding Trent Abernathy's supposed guilt.

"Derek's probably already contacted Cade," I said. "But it probably couldn't hurt to give him a call and let him know, just in case."

My assistant grinned. "It's the first thing I'm going to do when I get home."

I smiled back—what else could I do?—and decided that was as good an ending place as any. Key in hand, I went to lock the front door, and then the two of us walked out through the stock room, where I paused to set the alarm and headed outside. Through it all, I did my best to act calm and collected, but I couldn't help worrying about what was going to come next.

Had Cinderella been this nervous when anticipating her first ball?

I'd just have to hope I wouldn't want to turn into a pumpkin by the time the night was over.

Chapter 13

Disenchanted Evening

While I was driving home, I got a text from Malcolm. My first thought was that he was bailing on me at the last minute, but then I glanced at the screen.

Left Boston 15 minutes ago. Should be there in around 45.

Should I be relieved that I wasn't going to be stood up?

My thoughts on the subject of Malcolm Grimes were probably a little more complicated than that.

I touched the message to give it the thumbs-up emoji, although I didn't have time to make more of a reply than that, not while I was driving. Still, it would signal that I'd gotten his text and had some idea of the timing involved.

Milo and Lexi and Edgar were hanging out in

the living room when I got home, although they all seemed happy enough to head outside once I opened the back door for them. Once again, I couldn't shake the feeling that the raven was somehow disappointed in me and that he'd been expecting some more insight on my part.

But whatever he'd been trying to tell me, it hadn't gotten through. Or rather, I'd understood enough to realize he was actually angry with Sally and not me, and unfortunately, there wasn't a whole heck of a lot I could do about it.

Well, except be as friendly and kind to Edgar as I could. Not for the first time, I was very glad to have the two dogs there, since they were able to provide company for him and also act as sort of a buffer between him and humans. It didn't seem as though he'd tried to confide in them, either, although that was probably more because they'd be even less effective at interpreting the runes than I was.

But with all three of them outside for at least the next ten or fifteen minutes, I was able to go upstairs and pull out the makeup I'd bought a while back because it had seemed like a good idea at the time, even though I hardly ever wore it. A smoky eye palette, brow powder, the works. I still had no idea what my costume was going to be—it seemed that Malcolm Grimes liked his surprises—but I figured anything heavier than my usual mascara and lip gloss was probably a good idea for a nighttime event like this one.

However, I had to hope he didn't expect me to dress up like a Smurf or something. No way was I painting myself blue.

But I dabbed on some neutral brown eyeshadow and black liner, played up my brows a bit, and smoothed on a warm brick-red lipstick that my mother had always said was the perfect color for me but I was always too chicken to wear on anything except the most special occasions. When I was done, I mostly looked like myself...just a version of me who took a lot more care with her appearance than I ever did.

Wrangling my unruly waves took more time, but since I was only trying to create a more structured curl with the iron and not flat-iron my hair into submission, it mostly behaved. However, I was extremely glad that my weather spell seemed to be holding, because one stray rain shower and all those happy barrel waves would turn into one big frizzy mess.

I'd just unplugged the curling iron when the doorbell rang downstairs. By then, all the animals were back in the living room—telling me that Lexi and Milo had succeeded in coaxing Edgar through the dog door.

Normally, that would have been great. On the

other hand, I didn't think I was up to the task of explaining a pet raven to Malcolm Grimes.

"Can you all hang out in the kitchen for a bit?" I said breathlessly as I entered the room. "You might be kind of a lot to explain to my guest."

Milo cocked an eyebrow. "You never had to explain us to Noah," he pointed out.

Well, that was true. But Noah was a vet, and it was because of Milo that we'd even gotten together. Springing all three animals on Malcolm at the same time was an entirely different situation.

"I know," I said. "But it's not like I'm locking you in there. You all can come back out after we've left for the dance."

None of them looked particularly heartened by that explanation, but at least they all trooped off to the kitchen without any further arguments. Their departure allowed me to hurry for the door and open it to reveal Malcolm waiting there, several cloth garment bags draped over one arm. He was dressed simply, in a black crewneck sweater and jeans, but still managed to look every inch the handsome college professor, the kind a bunch of his undergrads probably would have had a crush on.

"Sorry about that," I told him. "I was upstairs when you rang the bell."

"It's fine," he replied. He didn't look too annoyed by the delay, luckily.

I stepped aside to let him in, and he sent an appraising glance over the living room. Although I'd done my best to tidy it up the day before, all the cleaning in the world couldn't hide the scratches on the coffee table or the obvious wear on the leather couch. Looking at damage I mostly ignored because I saw it every day, I realized it was kind of stupid to hide the animals when it was clear I couldn't have caused all that wear by myself.

"Charming," he observed, expression both approving and interested. "Eighteen-thirties or twenties, correct?"

"You know your architecture," I said with a smile. "Yes, the original house is dated to 1828, but it's been added onto so many times over the years that it's gotten hard to remember where the old bits leave off and the new ones begin."

"Old houses are a hobby of mine," he replied. "Of course, that's an easy enough hobby to have in New England. My own home isn't nearly as historical, though—it was built around 1900."

Still pretty old by a lot of standards, especially in a country that just loved to pull down historic buildings and put up strip malls. I remembered how I'd read that Malcolm's family had a lot of money, and wondered if they'd made their fortune in the railroads, or maybe in steel. If that was the case, then it made sense they'd have a family home that had been built at the tail end of the Gilded Age.

Obviously, I wasn't going to ask him about any of that. Inquiring about a family's wealth was rude enough at the best of times, let alone on a first date, and I certainly didn't want Malcolm to know I'd been researching him online.

Instead, I directed my attention toward the garment bags he was holding. "So, is it time for the big reveal?"

His dark eyes glinted. "I suppose I've kept you in suspense long enough. Here's yours."

He handed over the topmost bag, which felt fairly heavy. It seemed my worries about wearing some mortifyingly skimpy costume had been unfounded, although I needed to peek inside to be sure.

When I unzipped the bag, I saw a lot of gleaming ivory fabric with pearl edging. Dangling from the hanger was a small oval cap, also dotted with faux pearls. It was the only thing I even halfway recognized, because it reminded me of a costume piece I'd seen in a local production of *Romeo and Juliet* years ago.

Had he seriously thought it would be a good idea to dress up as the doomed Shakespearean lovers? If nothing else, we were a little too old to portray those characters.

My mystification must have been clear, because

he chuckled and unzipped the garment bag he still held, revealing a red velvet doublet and matching breeches, along with a drapey piece of fabric I thought might be a short cape.

"From *Faust*," he explained. "My costume is Mephistopheles, and yours is Marguerite. Alicia thought the costumes would be fun for a Halloween ball, and the Marguerite gown was your size."

I didn't know much about Faust. Wasn't he the guy who sold his soul to the devil?

Interesting that Malcolm had chosen the devil's costume, and not Faust's. Then again, that decision could have been based on what fit him and nothing else.

But the Marguerite gown was gorgeous...and about the farthest thing from skimpy. The hardest part would probably be figuring out how to get it on.

"It's beautiful," I said. "Thank you so much for loaning it to me—I know I wouldn't have been able to find anything this nice locally."

"Glad I could help," Malcolm replied. "And really, since it was my idea to go to the dance at the last minute, I would have been remiss if I hadn't at least tried to find something for you. But now I think we should probably get changed."

Good idea, since I didn't know how long it was going to take me to climb into the Marguerite gown. "You can use the bathroom downstairs," I said, and pointed toward the hallway. "I'll go up to my room to change."

For one awkward moment, I wondered what I would do if he asked me to call out if I needed help. To my relief, though, he only nodded and headed toward the bathroom I'd indicated.

That was my cue to go upstairs and close the door to my bedroom, then pull the costume out of its bag so I could see what I was working with. There was the gown itself, made of a beautiful ivory damask with those faux pearls sewn on the bodice, but then there was also a filmy underdress of sheer cotton and separate sleeves, heavily decorated in gold embroidery and more faux pearls, that appeared to tie on.

At least the gown didn't lace up the back like a lot of the historical dresses I'd seen in local museums, but instead had a series of industrial-strength snaps. I reminded myself that this was a theatrical costume, and therefore some authenticity had to be thrown out the window for the sake of quick changes between scenes.

Somehow I managed to shove myself into the thing, and even got the sleeves tied in place so they wouldn't start sliding down my arms.

I had to admit the overall effect was a lot more fabulous than I'd been expecting. The woman staring back at me from the mirror looked more like a fairytale princess than regular boring Charity Hughes, whose wardrobe generally consisted of black, black, and more black.

My hair felt a little casual, though, so I went into the bathroom, fished out some bobby pins, and pulled the front sections of my hair away from my face and up into a little bun while leaving the rest down.

Yes, that worked. I doubted any of it was truly period-correct, but this was a Halloween ball, after all. It wasn't as though I was being nitpicked by a bunch of overly zealous Revolutionary War reenactors.

I headed downstairs, where Malcolm was already waiting for me, probably because his costume was a lot less complicated than mine. He hadn't bothered with Mephistopheles' trademark goatee, but he had drawn on a thin little Vincent Price mustache that gave much the same effect.

"You look exquisite," he said as I approached.

Heat touched my cheeks, but I managed to sound casual enough as I said, "I'm just hoping I don't trip over myself all night long."

He chuckled then. "I'm sure you'll do fine."

I still wasn't too sure about that. It wasn't that I never wore dresses or skirts, but none of them were as long as this one, which I guessed had been made for someone slightly taller than I was.

But since I didn't have any heels that would be

remotely suitable for the dress, I'd just have to do my best to avoid falling flat on my face the second I started to move. The dress hadn't come with matching shoes, but luckily, I had a pair of pale gold flats that I'd bought years ago and never gotten around to donating still sitting in the back of my closet, and I'd dug them out and slid them on.

The costume hadn't come with a bag, either, but I'd stuffed my keys and I.D. and lipstick into a small beaded purse I'd bought for Grace's daughter's wedding, and I thought it worked okay. I fished out my keys now, saying, "Ready to head out?"

"Absolutely," Malcolm replied.

I locked up and followed him down the path, where one of the most gorgeous vintage cars I'd ever seen waited at the curb, all low-slung and a delectable British racing green. "That's yours?" I asked, even though I really didn't know who else's it could have been.

"Yes," he said with a smile, going over to the passenger door so he could open it for me. "Jaguar XK120. I don't usually drive it this much of a distance, but it looked like the weather was holding, so I thought I'd take it out for a spin."

Once again, I thanked my weather spell for doing such a good job of keeping the rain at bay. Not that I'd ever been into cars—as anyone who'd seen me driving my beat-up Land Rover could attest—but cars like this one went past being mere vehicles into true works of art.

The interior was camel-colored leather, just as luscious as the green exterior. It was a little difficult to jam the skirts of my gown and its underdress into the footwell, but Malcolm patiently waited until I was done before he slid behind the wheel.

That image made me want to smile, mostly because I could well believe that if Mephistopheles suddenly appeared on earth, this was exactly the kind of car he'd want to drive.

The engine started with a throaty rumble, and Malcolm slowly pulled away from the curb. Even with the rain holding back, it was still too cold to drive with the top down, and I found myself regretting that just the teensiest bit. Yes, going full convertible would have destroyed my hair, but on the other hand, it would have allowed all my neighbors to see me driving down the street in a car that looked like it should be in a museum, not cruising along Winter Island Drive.

We headed for Mercy Tavern, where I would have felt self-conscious walking inside in this garb if it weren't that it looked as though quite a few couples had also stopped here to grab a drink before heading to the ball. I saw witches and vampires and fairies and all sorts of historical clothing, although none of it seemed quite as fancy as what Malcolm and I were wearing.

I hadn't thought it was possible to get reservations if you were just going to the bar, but my companion must have finagled something, because we were immediately led to a small table off to the side rather than having to jockey for a spot in the crowded space.

"This is great," I said as I sank into my chair. "I thought for sure we'd have to wait."

His dark eyes twinkled. "I might have made a few arrangements."

About what I'd expected. I wouldn't press for details, though, mainly because I didn't want him to think I was impressed by the way he'd used his money to get everything to go smoothly this evening.

Our server came up to us then, a girl named Jenny who'd waited on Noah and me a few times. I could tell she was startled by my companion because of the way her eyes widened for a second, but she was completely professional as she inquired as to our orders.

Malcolm asked for a martini, and I requested a glass of white wine. No sense in getting too crazy.

His mouth quirked slightly as I placed my order, but he didn't say anything.

"How was traffic?" I asked, and again I saw that lift at the corner of his lips, as though he was amused by the obvious change of subject.

"It was fine," he replied. "I made good time. It

seems as though a lot of the crowds up here have gone."

"Most of them," I said. "Some stayed behind for the ball, but after tomorrow, things will really thin out."

Jenny came back with our drinks, and I was grateful for that. I'd wanted to tell Malcolm about this latest development with Trent Abernathy, but I hadn't wanted to broach the subject until I was sure we wouldn't be overheard.

"The police arrested someone for Eunice Bartlett's death this afternoon," I said, and Malcolm, who'd just taken a swallow of his martini, didn't quite choke but still gulped it down a bit more precipitously than he'd probably planned.

"They did?" he replied. "What happened?"

So I explained how Sage and I and the rest of the people in my store—and up and down the block, most likely—had watched the police swarm Trent's store and then march out with him a few minutes later, and how Derek had called me a while later to fill me in on the details.

"It sounds like they've got pretty concrete evidence," I went on. "So I guess we can all stop worrying about finding the killer."

"That's wonderful news," Malcolm replied. "I'm sure everyone was on edge, not knowing who the murderer really was."

I nodded and finally sipped some of my

chardonnay. "That's for sure. I still have no idea what Trent's motive could have been, but I assume it'll come out at some point. To be honest, he always kind of gave me the creeps. Not to the point where I would have ever suspected him of being capable of murder, but...."

"But you're not entirely surprised, either," Malcolm supplied.

"Not as much as I would have been if it had been someone else." I was still holding my wine glass, and I swirled the contents a bit before adding, "Even though we have some closure now, the whole thing is kind of appalling. Sage says Cade is having a real rough time of it."

"Your assistant knows Cade Bartlett?"

Malcolm sounded surprised, but I didn't think his reaction was too odd. After all, it wasn't as though Cade's and Sage's paths would have ever crossed if his mother hadn't been killed right behind the shop.

"He came in to talk to her, since she was the one who first found Eunice," I explained. "And because it sounds as though he doesn't have much of a support network, she's been sort of a shoulder for him to lean on."

"That's kind of her," Malcolm said, a note of sympathy in his tone.

"She's a kind person. It seems like they've hit it off, which is nice. I mean, I don't expect Sage to make Cade forget all about what happened to his mother, but on the other hand, giving him something else to think about can only be a good thing."

Malcolm made a sound of agreement, and after that, the conversation moved on to less weighty subjects, like how the costumes we were wearing had come from a production of *Faust* the college had put on a couple of years ago, and how he'd decided on them because the measurements for Mephistopheles' and Marguerite's costumes worked so well for us.

"I suppose we didn't have to wear costumes that were at all related to one another," he added. "But it just seemed more fun to have ones that were."

"I agree," I said. "And this is really a beautiful dress. I know I wouldn't have been able to find anything as nice."

Jenny came by then and asked if we wanted anything else, and we both demurred since the hour was quickly approaching seven and we needed to drive over to the Hawthorne Hotel, where the dance was being held. Honestly, it was so close that we probably could have walked—if we'd been wearing street clothes. As it was, I knew parking spaces would be hotly contested, so it just seemed better to get there a little before the doors opened.

Malcolm left a couple of twenties on the table —much more than was probably necessary—and we headed out to climb into the Jag and cruise over to the hotel. As I'd feared, the parking lot was already almost at capacity, but he managed to snag one of the few remaining spots, thus banishing any fears that we might have to walk for blocks after all.

A line already extended from the hotel's side door, the one that opened onto the parking lot. I guessed the management wanted to make sure their fancy front entrance wasn't blocked for anyone who was staying there and wasn't attending the ball, which made sense. And while under other circumstances it might have felt a little less special to be entering the event that way, the organizers had done their best to dress up the spot, with black gauze draped around the doorway and black lights highlighting oversized spiders and hanging witches on broomsticks.

Malcolm and I got behind a couple who looked as though they'd gone full-on fae for the event, with gauzy wings and lots of glitter and costumes that maybe were supposed to be Oberon and Titania but seemed mostly an excuse to show a lot of skin. Not for the first time, I was very glad that the dress I wore was so modest. Yes, it revealed just a bit of cleavage, and that was enough for me. I never thought of myself as being particularly prudish, but I also didn't see the point in letting it all hang out in public.

Also, the rain might be holding off, but it was still darn cold out there.

After what felt like an interminable wait but was probably only around ten minutes, the line began to move. When we got to the door, Malcolm produced a pair of tickets, and we were both given wristbands that would allow us to come and go if we found it necessary to leave the hall for some reason.

And while I'd been to the dance years ago, it seemed clear to me that the decorating committee had definitely stepped up their game during the intervening time. Enormous fake trees with bare branches lined the perimeter of the room, decked with fairy lights in shades of green and purple, while more black gauze had been tacked up to hide the ceiling. At one side of the room was the stage, empty at the moment but obviously waiting for a DJ to appear and take over the enormous banks of equipment.

At the other side of the room were the refreshment tables, also disguised with swags of black gauze and festoons of glittering black ivy leaves. It was worlds away from the proper-looking space that had been the site of numerous weddings and Women's League luncheons.

"Would you like a drink?" Malcolm asked, inclining his head toward the bar, which was hosted by a disreputable-looking zombie.

"No, I'm fine," I said hastily. While I would probably want another glass of wine before the night was over, I didn't think it would be a very good idea to add anything to the chardonnay I'd just drunk before I'd had a decent amount of time to let it burn off.

It didn't seem Malcolm had brought me here intending to get me drunk and have his wicked way with me, because he didn't appear too disappointed by my demurral. "Well, just let me know when you're ready. It's probably a good idea to get some water, though."

I told him that would be great, and he headed off for a refreshment table that held a big bowl of punch and a large beverage dispenser of water. While he was gone, I let my gaze move over the crowd, looking for anyone I might know. The odds weren't too huge, just because the event was popular with tourists, and even if it weren't, it wasn't as if I knew all of Salem's forty thousand-plus occupants.

From what I could tell, though—a lot of people wore masks, making any kind of identification that much more difficult—no one here was anyone I knew, and I allowed myself an inner sigh of relief. It wasn't as if there was anything wrong about appearing here with Malcolm, but I tried to be as private as I could about my personal life, and I didn't feel like fielding questions about the new man I was with.

Not that I was really "with" him. This was a casual date and nothing more.

All right, not so casual, I thought as I looked down at my damask skirts. It seemed the theme this year was supposed to be dark fairyland or something adjacent to that, but I got the impression that most people had gone with whatever costumes made them happy.

Malcolm came over to me, a plastic cup of water in each hand. I took one from him and murmured a thank you.

"There's some good people-watching here tonight," he commented, then sipped some of his water.

"Well, it's a Halloween dance," I replied. "I suppose that's kind of par for the course."

He grinned. In the dim lighting, that penciled-on Vincent Price made him look much more sinister, although his flash of a smile right then did a lot to dispel the impression. "I suppose that's true. Still, I can see why so many people go to an effort to come to this event. It's so much more than a costume party."

That was true. I had no idea how many hours it had taken the dance committee to transform this ballroom into an eerie fairyland, but I knew it wasn't anything that could have been done overnight. No, they'd probably started setting up the morning before at the very least.

I figured it was as good a time as any to ask the question that had been floating around in the back of my mind for a while. "So...how did you end up with an extra ticket to this thing, anyway?"

Maybe the slightest hesitation, and then he said, "I bought the tickets early this year when they first went on sale. At the time, I was seeing someone. We went our separate ways at the beginning of the summer, however. To be honest, I'd almost forgotten I had the tickets at all until I came to Salem to investigate Eunice's murder and saw the posters pinned up along Essex Street. And then I met you, and I thought it would be nice to take you...assuming you were game, of course."

"And I was," I replied with a smile, one that was accompanied by an inner smile of relief. The story seemed ordinary enough, and I could understand why he might have forgotten about the tickets until he had visible reminders practically shoved in his face.

"Yes, you were," he agreed, matching my smile with one of his own.

It seemed the people running the dance had decided there were enough people in the room to get the party started, because a man dressed in a pretty credible Frankenstein's monster costume approached the DJ stand and welcomed everyone, then immediately launched into "The Monster Mash."

Malcolm didn't ask me to dance, leading me to wonder if he'd mostly invited me here to hang out, or whether he was simply holding off for something a little less exuberant. That proved to be the case, because after waiting through "Pet Sematary" and "Love Potion No. 9," the DJ started to play "I Put on a Spell on You."

"Shall we?" Malcolm asked, and I swallowed. Not that I was the world's greatest dancer or anything close to it, but I would much rather have done something fast rather than a piece where we'd have to hold on to each other.

The moment had come, however, and I knew turning him down would be rude. It was just a dance—it wasn't like he was asking me to marry him or something.

"Sure," I replied.

Luckily, there was a bar-height table nearby where we could set down our half-drunk cups of water, so we left them there and made our way out to the crowded dance floor. His arms went around me, and I did my best not to flinch. Not because he was being grabby or anything close to it—I could tell he wasn't trying to pull me in too tight—but because this still felt way too intimate despite his caution.

How could I be out here dancing with another

man when Noah and I had just broken up a month earlier?

But I was dancing with Malcolm, and I certainly wasn't going to make a fool of myself by tearing away from his grasp and running off the dance floor. After all, this was part of moving on, wasn't it? You met someone who seemed at least sort of compatible, and you took a few steps into the waters of a new relationship, letting yourself get used to the temperature, the way it wasn't quite what you were used to but might be fine nonetheless.

I had to admit he smelled good, of some kind of citrusy cologne or aftershave that hadn't been detectible until he was up close like this. And although his arms around me felt very different from Noah's, not as muscular, not as comforting in a way I'd never been able to exactly define, I told myself that was all right. Malcolm wasn't Noah, and I had to be okay with that.

A shift in the crowd as we turned, and then I saw a pair of blue eyes staring at me, eyes bright as laser beams despite the intentional dimness of the room.

My stomach fell.

Noah Jenkins.

He was standing at the edge of the dance floor, a woman I realized was his front office assistant Courtney at his side. She had on a nymph costume not too dissimilar from the one Sage had worn only a few days earlier, a crown of autumn leaves on her long blonde hair.

Noah, on the other hand, didn't look as though he'd made much of an effort to dress up, and was wearing a black suit and a black half mask. Those piercing blue eyes, though, were unmistakable, as was the wave of his brown hair away from his forehead.

What the hell was he doing here?

And with Courtney, of all people? Had he gone running into his assistant's arms immediately after our breakup, or had he at least waited a little while?

I had no idea. The crowds shifted again, blocking him from view, and I was glad for that. Even so, it couldn't erase what had just happened.

Noah had seen me at the dance with another man.

And you saw him with another woman, my brain poked at me, but for some silly reason, it didn't quite feel the same.

I forced myself back to the here and now, to the irony of dancing to a song about a man casting a magical spell when all we witches knew such a thing wasn't even possible. Magic passed through the female line, except for those rare—and terrible —instances when a boy child was born to a witch.

So at least I didn't have to worry about

Malcolm Grimes being a fellow practitioner of magic. No, he was just an ordinary man.

An ordinary distinguished, rich, handsome man.

On paper, he was perfect, right? Maybe a little too old for me, but since I'd just turned thirty the month before, it wasn't as if he was robbing the cradle or anything close to it.

But after seeing Noah right now—after having those blue eyes meet mine, eyes that were bluer and brighter than any other eyes I'd ever seen—I knew Malcolm didn't stand a chance.

All that had taken place in a split second. As far as I could tell, nothing had shifted in my expression...or maybe Malcolm just wasn't paying attention.

Mercifully, the song ended, and we went back to retrieve our cups of water. I didn't think he noticed anything, though. "It looks like they have a full house," he observed, a comment that a quick glance around the ballroom told me was accurate.

"They sell out every year," I said. "I think they've been trying to find a bigger venue, but there isn't much like that here in Salem."

"No, I suppose not," he replied.

Was that the slightest hint of condescension in his tone? It was hard for me to tell, because the DJ had just started playing Marilyn Manson's cover of

"Personal Jesus," and the decibel levels had definitely risen.

I supposed that Salem felt poky and small compared to Boston, but I wasn't going to comment on that. "And obviously, it's too chilly to have the dance outside in a big tent, the way some people have suggested."

"Yes, it's very inconvenient for Halloween to fall at the end of October," Malcolm said with a smile.

Despite my discomfort at his tone a moment earlier, I couldn't help returning that smile. I remembered all too well all those Halloweens when my mother and I had put together what felt like the perfect costume...only to have the effect utterly ruined by her insisting that I put a warm coat over the whole thing.

But I still loved that the holiday came during spooky season, with the leaves mostly fallen from the trees and their branches bare against a ghostly moon.

Our conversation was mundane enough after that as Malcolm and I spoke about our favorite Halloweens as children, although it sounded as though his had been quite different from mine, with lots of private parties rather than getting to ramble through his neighborhood the way I had.

Afterward, he excused himself to go to the restroom, and I lingered by the table, still nursing my cup of water and wondering if it would be time to get a real drink after this. My gaze scanned the room and then came to a dead halt.

Noah stood a few feet away, eyes fixed on me, with Courtney nowhere to be seen.

"Hey," he said.

"Hey," I replied, knowing how weak that single word sounded, even as I couldn't come up with anything wittier to say.

"Having a good time?" he asked, voice almost too casual.

There was a hell of a question. Up until a minute ago, I might have said I was having more fun than I would have expected. Now, though, as I looked back at the man I knew I still loved...would always love...I realized I'd been fooling myself.

"It's all right," I allowed. Then, since I figured things couldn't get much more awkward, I added, "So...you and Courtney?"

Something in his expression shifted. I couldn't say what exactly, because it was too dark in the ballroom to see much detail. But then he said, "No. She and her boyfriend bought the tickets, but he got food poisoning from a bad bratwurst. He told her to go ahead and come to the dance because she was really looking forward to it, so she called me and asked if I would use Jeff's ticket." Noah paused there and looked down at himself, mouth twisting in a lopsided smile. "It was kind of last minute, so I didn't exactly have a lot of time to put together a real costume."

Well, that explained the suit and the plain black mask. He'd probably grabbed the thing from the nearest CVS, figuring it was better than nothing.

"That was nice of you," I said, and he shrugged.

"You're looking pretty fancy," he went on. "Did you have that hiding in your closet all along?"

I couldn't help making a face. "Hardly. Malcolm teaches at Roxbury University, and he borrowed our outfits from the drama department there."

"Malcolm, huh?" Noah said, and I couldn't help feeling a tiny twinge of hope.

Could it be possible that he was jealous?

"I sort of met him in connection with Eunice Bartlett's murder," I explained. "And it turned out he had an extra ticket for the dance, so I was able to tag along."

There. I could only hope by describing the outing in the least date-like way possible, Noah would pick up that it wasn't as if I'd fallen right into a hot-and-heavy romance.

"That was nice of him," he said, but now something in his tone sounded almost absent. "Well, I shouldn't leave Courtney alone for too long. You have a nice evening."

"You, too."

And then he headed off into the crowd, while I did my best to hide my disappointment at his leaving. Yes, we were both here with other people, and yet...

...and yet, it had been really good to talk to him.

I could only hope his civility had come from a place of beginning to realize we should have tried to patch things up, and not simple politeness.

But I'd learned one thing. I had no idea what Malcolm was expecting of me—if anything—and yet I knew I couldn't provide it for him.

Not while Noah Jenkins was still around.

Chapter 14

Doin' Time

The rest of the evening was fairly uneventful. I danced a few more times with Malcolm, stood in the crowd next to him while we all watched a group of tribal dancers take the stage for a while, and even had another glass of wine. By then, enough time had elapsed since my drink at Mercy Tavern that I didn't feel any real effects from the merlot at all, which was just as well. I didn't think my "date" had noticed anything strange after he came back from his trip to the bathroom, but I also didn't want to get so tipsy that something unintended might slip out by accident.

It was a little before midnight when Malcolm drove me home in his gleaming dark green Jag. And although he got out to escort me to the door, I could tell right away that he didn't plan to end the evening with a kiss. No, he only told me he'd had a good time—a sentiment I echoed—and then said he'd come back to Salem the following week to pick up my borrowed costume.

"Because it's late, and I don't want to have to make you change," he said. "Alicia assured me that they aren't going to need these costumes at all this season, so there's no hurry. Oh, and she wanted to let you know that she'll take care of taking it to the dry cleaner—she has an arrangement with someone local who's used to working with unusual fabrics."

That was a relief—and very kind of her, since I'd been wondering where I would take the dress to get cleaned. Also, it had been one thing to change out of our street clothes and into our costumes while it was still broad daylight and we didn't have an entire evening behind us, but I knew it would have felt strange to do such a thing now.

"Good," I said, then paused. "Thanks for taking me to the ball. I had a really good time."

Had I, though? Overall, the evening just felt weird to me, even though nothing strange had occurred. Probably I was just off-balance after bumping into Noah like that.

"So did I," Malcolm replied, a hint of a smile lifting one corner of his mouth. "I'll be in touch."

And then he inclined his head toward me

before heading back to his car, jaunty in his blood-red doublet and breeches.

Although the car had performed seamlessly all night, I still waited on the doorstep to make sure the engine started okay. Once it had growled its way to life—and after Malcolm had begun to back out of the driveway—I went inside and locked the door behind me.

Milo and Lexi and Edgar were in the living room. If they'd been asleep before my arrival, it seemed the sound of my key in the lock had been enough to wake them up, because they all appeared alert enough as I came in and set my little evening bag on the table next to the sofa.

"It's late," Milo said, tone almost but not quite accusing.

"It's not even midnight yet," I replied. "Cinderella got home before she turned into a pumpkin."

The confused glances the animals gave each other told me they had no idea who Cinderella was, and I couldn't help smiling as I eased off my golden flats. They'd done a good job tonight, but they also weren't broken in all the way, and my toes were screaming for relief.

"Did you have fun?" Lexi asked.

"It was...interesting," I said.

The dogs looked at each other again, while

across the room, Edgar tilted his head to one side. I assumed he'd been listening to the whole exchange, but because he'd never met Noah, he wasn't as worried about me moving on with a new partner as Lexi and Milo were.

"Interesting how?" Milo pressed. "Did he kiss you goodnight?"

I just had to laugh then. Who knew that having the two dogs around was almost as bad as dealing with my mother when it came to my love life?

"No, he did not," I replied, and was further amused by the expressions of obvious relief that passed across my canine companions' faces. "I have a feeling that Malcolm and I are going to be friends and nothing more."

I stopped there, however, thinking it probably would be better not to mention how I'd bumped into Noah at the dance. The last thing I wanted to do was get the dogs' hopes up.

Even though mine had lifted more than they probably should have.

"Anyway," I went on, "it's late, and I want to go to sleep. Do any of you need to go outside one last time?"

Lexi and Milo both shook their heads. "No, we went out after we had our dinner," Lexi told me. "Edgar's been sleeping most of the time, so I don't think he probably needs to."

I glanced over at the raven. He cracked one

eyelid but otherwise didn't seem inclined to make much of a response.

Which was fine. I still didn't quite know what was going on with the raven—bird psychology wasn't exactly my forte, since I hadn't dealt with many avian familiars—but he definitely seemed down to me. Whether it was full-on depression or just disappointment that he hadn't been able to communicate effectively with me, I couldn't say for sure.

At least he was ready to get up from his little nest on the couch when I approached, and to land on my exposed wrist—no way would I let those claws get anywhere near the shoulder of the costume I wore—so I could carry him upstairs. The dogs trailed behind, and then it was time to remove the gorgeous Marguerite gown and take down my hair.

"Goodnight, Cinderella," I murmured to my reflection in the mirror.

Tonight might have been all about fantasy and make-believe, but tomorrow I needed to get back to work.

We all slept in, though, which was probably a good thing. Sundays were generally my lazy days where I got caught up with laundry and any other household chores that might have been neglected during the week, but with the dance behind me, I needed to turn my attention to Eunice Bartlett's murder.

A lot of people probably would have commented that doing so was a waste of my time, considering how Trent Abernathy was now locked up for that very crime. However, I couldn't ignore the way my gut kept telling me something else was going on here, and that meant I needed to pick away at the problem as best I could. If he was innocent, I had to find some way to exonerate him.

My attempt at using the scrying mirror to figure out the crime hadn't helped me very much, so instead I thought I'd try the Tarot. I'd say my luck using the cards was fifty percent at best, but fifty percent was better than nothing.

After letting the animals outside—the clouds of the day before had disappeared without shedding a single drop of rain, and the sky this morning was a hard, bright blue—I sat down at the kitchen table with my Rider-Waite deck and a cup of peppermint tea, hoping the combination would be enough to clear my thoughts and guide me to, if not a solution, at least a couple of clues that might help me to find my way.

I shuffled the deck and shuffled it again. My mother had always said she could sense when the cards knew it was time to stop, but I wasn't that gifted in their use. All I could do was shuffle and shuffle, and then, when I knew I couldn't delay any longer, lay down a card and see what it had to tell me.

Well, there was a doozy.

The Tower was never a good card to pull, even though some people tried to say it was more a card about transformation than anything else. However, its main meaning was sudden, violent upheaval—which was sort of what you'd expect if you'd been brutally murdered out of the blue.

After the Tower came the Four of Pentacles, reversed. I had to pause and pull out my little cheat sheet for Tarot because I couldn't remember what that was even supposed to mean.

Over-spending, greed, self-protection.

Nothing I'd heard about Eunice Bartlett had made it sound as though she was an extravagant person. So was the card talking about her killer?

Maybe. I supposed some people could have called Trent Abernathy greedy, thanks to the way he always tried to hoover up whatever even slightly arcane objects crossed his path. Still, though, the definition didn't seem to fit his situation very well.

The Tarot wasn't infallible, though. Also, if I was correct in my suspicions regarding his guilt and Trent was just someone who'd happened to be in the wrong place at the wrong time, then the Four of Pentacles wasn't referring to him at all, but the as-yet-known killer.

I reached for my cup of peppermint tea and took a sip. Whether or not it would really help to clarify my thoughts, I didn't know, but at least it tasted good going down.

Time for the final card. In general, I tried to do three-card spreads, just because they got me to the heart of a matter without wasting much time, but if none of this seemed to make much sense, I'd try for something different, maybe even a Celtic Cross, although I knew I'd have to look up how to do it since it had been years since I'd attempted one.

The Ten of Swords.

Oh, boy.

It was upright, but in the world of the Tarot, that was worse than being reversed. The card generally indicated betrayal, crisis...deep wounds and painful endings.

Well, Eunice Bartlett had suffered a very painful ending, that was for sure.

Unfortunately, the group of cards hadn't told me much that I didn't already know. The betrayal part, though...that got me thinking.

Had Eunice known her killer?

I supposed it was likely that she and Trent had known each other simply because of their interests and areas of specialty. Eunice was more focused on witches, true, but Trent claimed to have witch-related artifacts in his shop, including an ancient set of manacles he swore had been used in the

Salem witch trials. I wasn't so sure about that—most items connected to the infamous case of mass hysteria were now ensconced in our town's witch museum and not offered for five figures to unsuspecting tourists—and yet he swore up and down that they were real.

But even though it would have been easy enough to claim a connection between Trent and Eunice, I honestly didn't believe that was the case here.

Betrayal. Who had betrayed whom? Had Eunice been involved in some kind of deal that had gone horribly wrong?

As soon as the thought crossed my mind, I wanted to dismiss it. We were talking about a retired history professor here, not El Chapo. But at the same time, I couldn't ignore the ugly fact that someone had felt compelled to murder her in a messy, violent kind of way behind my store. It wasn't as though someone had tipped some arsenic into her tea or anything.

I hadn't heard anything from Derek following our conversation the afternoon before...not that I'd expected to. It was the weekend, after all, and although I didn't have his schedule memorized or anything, I'd gotten the impression that he didn't work most Saturdays and Sundays unless something came up, like the raid on Trent's store.

And all I had was Derek's office number.

Except....

I rose from my chair and went in search of my purse. After I got out my wallet, I extracted his business card from the compartment where I'd stowed it and then unlocked my phone so I could take a look at my call log from the day before.

Yes, there was Derek's call, coming in around 4:15.

The number didn't match the one on the card, which seemed to indicate he must have been calling from his personal cell phone.

I hesitated. True, it was now after ten, so I wouldn't be breaking any rules of courtesy by trying to contact him now. On the other hand, this was his day off, and I didn't know whether I should be bugging him over something that wasn't much more than a hunch.

Well, at least I could find out whether Trent was still in jail or whether the judge had granted him bail after all.

A quick peek out the kitchen window told me that Milo and Lexi and Edgar were still enjoying the November sunshine, the two dogs lying on a patch of frost-yellowed grass, the raven perched in the now-bare oak tree to one side of the yard. From what I could tell, none of them seemed inclined to go anywhere any time soon.

Before I could lose my nerve, I touched the screen to initiate a call to the number from the afternoon before. A moment later, Derek's voice came through the speaker.

"Charity? Is everything okay?"

"It's fine," I assured him. He'd sounded startled to hear from me, so I wanted to make sure he knew this wasn't anything too urgent. "I just—I've been thinking about Trent's arrest yesterday. Was he granted bail?"

"No, the judge denied it, just as I thought," Derek replied, now sounding somewhat mystified. "He'll be held in jail until the trial. Why?"

"Because I'd like to talk to him, if that's okay," I said. "I know this is going to sound strange, but I have this gut feeling that he's not the killer."

A long silence. Was Derek thinking of ways to gently shoot me down, to tell me I wouldn't be allowed to talk to the suspect because I wasn't family or legal counsel?

When he spoke, though, he sounded brisk enough. "I know you've had some luck in the past figuring out murders, but I really don't think you're going to turn up anything new here. We found the murder weapon in Abernathy's shop, and forensic analysis confirmed that it had Eunice Bartlett's DNA on it."

I hadn't known about that. Clearly, the investigation had carried on apace while I was off dancing with Malcolm Grimes at the Halloween ball.

And even though this all probably seemed like a done deal, I wasn't going to give up so easily.

"That does sound pretty bad," I allowed. "But who's to say the evidence wasn't planted there?"

"That's what Abernathy's been saying the whole time," Derek replied, now sounding grimly amused. "But it doesn't mean it isn't true."

"I suppose he could be lying," I said. "On the other hand, he could be innocent and doing his best to point out the only real defense he has. Would it really be that big a deal for me to go talk to him? Or is that not allowed?"

"It's allowed," Derek said. "Only two visitors per day, but it's not like anyone is going to be beating down his door to visit him on a Sunday, especially his defense attorney. Let me call the station and talk to the deputy on duty at the jail, and I'll see what I can do."

"Thanks, Derek," I replied, and meant it. Maybe, since Trent was being allowed visitors, all I would have had to do was walk into the station and request an interview. However, I couldn't help thinking the whole process would go a lot smoother if I had Derek set it up for me.

"Give me a few minutes."

I told him that was fine, and we ended the call there. No point in going off to start something else, not when I didn't know for sure when he was going to get back in touch. Instead, I sat down again and finished my cup of peppermint tea, even as I continued to gaze at the trio of cards on the table.

The Tower. The Four of Pentacles. The Ten of Swords. If I'd pulled that same set of cards while doing a reading for a friend—not that I actually would have done such a thing, not when pretty much everyone in my coven was much better at this sort of thing than I was—I would have told them to watch their back, that all sorts of horrible stuff might be coming down the pike.

But it was way too late for Eunice. All I could do now was try my best to make sure the right person was behind bars.

———————

Derek called me back about ten minutes later to let me know he'd set it up with the deputies on duty and that they'd be expecting me.

"I honestly don't think you're going to learn anything new," he said. "But if you do, give me a call."

"I will," I promised. The least I could do was share my findings with him, considering how helpful he'd been through this whole mess.

Well, unless I discovered something witchy about the situation, in which case I'd have to be a lot more careful about what I said.

We ended the call, and I put down my phone so I could go over to the back door and look outside. The dogs were now up and about, sniffing at various plants, although it didn't look as though Edgar planned to give up his roost in the oak tree any time soon.

"I need to run an errand," I told Milo and Lexi as they came trotting over to the back stoop. "It probably shouldn't take very long. All the same, it's probably better if you stay inside while I'm gone."

"Sure," Milo replied. "We've been out for a while, so it's okay to be in the house."

"We were getting ready to come inside anyway," Lexi added.

Well, at least I wouldn't be depriving them of some precious outdoor time. I looked over at Edgar where he sat in the tree and lifted my arm, and immediately he flapped his wings and took flight, landing on my outstretched limb only a moment later.

We went inside, and I made sure to check their water before I left. No real worries about lunch, not when I guessed I would only be gone for forty-five minutes or so at the most, which would get me back to the house well before noon.

"Be good," I said, and Milo cocked his head at me.

"When aren't we?" he returned, tone almost

plaintive, so I bent down and patted him on the head.

"You're right—you're always good," I told him. "But now, I need to get going."

After slipping my purse over my shoulder, I let myself out the back door and locked it. There had been plenty of times when I'd left that door unsecured, just because I knew my neighborhood was completely safe and I'd been in a hurry.

Now, though, since I couldn't know for sure whether Eunice Bartlett's killer was still out there somewhere, I thought it better to be cautious.

A deputy escorted me to an interview room once I arrived at the station, rather than take me to Trevor Abernathy's cell. That was fine; I noticed that the room was watched by a closed-circuit camera, and when Trent was brought in, handcuffed, the deputy who'd escorted him stationed himself near the door.

Clearly, this interview wasn't going to be as private as I'd hoped. Then again, I realized the police would never leave a suspected murderer alone with a member of the public, even if he might have been handcuffed.

And it wasn't as though I'd planned to discuss anything witchy with Trent. I just wanted to get his side of the story, along with any reasons he might have for protesting that the chunk of pyrite with Eunice Bartlett's DNA on it had been planted at his store.

A flicker of surprise showed in his light gray eyes when he sat down opposite me. From that reaction, I guessed he'd been told he had a visitor, but not who it was.

"Hi, Trent," I said. "I was hoping we could chat a bit."

He settled himself against the back of the hard plastic chair where he sat, his handcuffs jingling faintly as he did so. "About what?"

His expression was hard, and I supposed I couldn't blame him for that. It wasn't as though we'd ever been friends or anything close to it. I still didn't know exactly how old he was, but I guessed he must be somewhere in his middle or late fifties, hair that had once been fair now mostly silver-gray. In contrast, his skin was ruddy and heavily lined, as if he'd spent most of his early years outdoors before deciding to open a curiosity shop.

"I don't think you killed Eunice Bartlett," I said boldly. "So I guess I just wanted to talk to you and get your side of things."

One silvery eyebrow lifted. "Why don't you think I did it? The cops sure do."

"Because as far as I can tell, you didn't have any

reason to kill her," I replied. "I mean, did you even know her?"

"We talked a couple of times about the stuff in my shop," he said, tone wary, as though he wanted to make sure he thought over his response before he allowed it to escape his lips. "But I never met her in person. We just talked on the phone."

That little piece of information sounded promising. "So...would you have even known what she looked like?"

"Nope," he said. "And that's what I told the cops, but they didn't want to hear it. Said I could've looked up a picture of her online and didn't need to have seen her in person."

Well, that made some sense. Still, I didn't know whether a jury would think that little tidbit wasn't important.

Not that I wanted this to go to trial. I wanted to get it figured out so I wouldn't have to look over my shoulder every time I went outside to put something in that damn dumpster.

"We can leave that part for now," I told him. "What was this about the pyrite they found in your store?"

Trent's pale eyes narrowed. "You sure know a lot about this case for someone who isn't a cop, Charity."

Yes, I did. As smoothly as I could, I replied, "I'm friends with Detective Falco. Also, I have a particular interest because of where Eunice Bartlett died. I don't like the idea of the real killer being out there somewhere when it's clear they like to use the back of my shop as their killing ground."

No real reaction. Trent sat there for a moment, staring at me out of those mist-gray eyes, and I wondered if this had been a complete waste of time. As far as I was able to tell, he didn't seem to have much interest in talking to me at all.

But then he leaned forward, brows pulling together as he said, "I know that rock wasn't mine. I don't sell stuff like that unless you want to count those crystal skulls from South America. Someone must have put it there."

"'Someone' being the real killer."

He nodded, the set of his shoulders just a little less tense than it had been a moment earlier. It seemed to me that he'd been expecting me to be less than receptive to his theories and had thought I'd openly scoff at the idea that he might have been framed.

But I couldn't help thinking the same thing, which was why I wanted to get as much information from him as I could.

"Do you have any idea when that might have happened?" I asked, and his mouth tightened.

"Not really," he replied. "I mean, it had to have been sometime during the past week, because I try to go around and dust everything every other week and I'd last done it right before all the tourists really started showing up for Halloween. If it had been there when I was cleaning, then I would have noticed it. My store might look like a junk shop to a lot of people, but I know what I have in there... and what I don't."

A week was still a lot of time. However, I guessed that the stone must have appeared soon after Eunice's death, just so the killer could make sure it was there when the police came knocking.

Which I supposed begged the question of why the killer hadn't immediately called in the anonymous tip that had led the authorities to Trent's shop. I couldn't answer that question, though, not without a lot more information than I currently had on hand.

"Did they find your fingerprints on the rock?"

He shook his head. "No. And that's because I never touched the damn thing, or noticed it before they were bagging it for evidence. I tried to tell your Detective Falco that, and he only said I must have used gloves when I handled it."

A plausible enough theory, but I knew it was wrong. Of course Trent had never handled the piece of pyrite. It wasn't his, and had been hidden in the jumbled chaos of his store until the killer had decided it was time to spring the trap.

"Did you notice anyone strange in your shop

this past week?" I asked next. "Anyone who might have been lingering near that spot?"

Now he smiled, showing yellowed teeth. "It was Halloween week. What do you think?"

I couldn't help smiling in return. He was right—pretty much all of us shopkeepers on Essex Street had been slammed by the tourists coming to Salem for Halloween. The idea that one of them would have stood out in all that noise was kind of silly...unless the person involved had done something to truly make themselves obvious.

And clearly, that was the last thing the killer would have wanted to do.

Before I could say anything, Trent spoke again.

"I appreciate you wanting to help. And I keep hoping that the judge will decide the evidence is too circumstantial and will throw out the whole case. But right now, I'm pretty sure the only thing that'll make all this go away is if the killer decides to turn themselves in...and I don't see that happening any time soon. Do you?"

I wished I had words of encouragement I could give him. From where I sat, though, it seemed as if every possible angle was something the murderer had already thought of.

So I made myself stare back at him and say, "I don't know, Trent. I just don't know."

I got in my SUV and drove home, feeling dejected. All along, I'd been so sure Trent Abernathy was in possession of the single piece of information that, when mentioned to me, would make the solution to the problem crystal clear.

There was a joke. The whole situation felt muddier than ever.

At least the traffic was pretty light, as though most of the tourists who'd stuck it out for the Halloween ball had gotten on the road and left Salem to us locals. I knew that wasn't entirely accurate—we were never completely free of visitors here, even during the cold, dark winter months when sightseeing could be more of a chore than anything else—but still, there was very little drama on my drive home.

Good thing, because I knew I was distracted, my brain going over everything Trent had said during our little interview, just in case something might occur to me that hadn't been immediately apparent when we were talking.

Unfortunately, I didn't have any flashes of inspiration.

No, I had basically nothing at all.

I pulled into my driveway and got out, slanting an upward look at the sky. The clear, perfect blue from this morning was rapidly disappearing, with dark clouds moving in from the northeast.

If it wanted to rain, I wouldn't stop it this time.

Key in the lock, and then I was inside...and paused in shock. My Tarot cards, which I'd left sitting on the kitchen table, were now scattered across the living room.

"We tried to stop him," Milo told me. He'd come running over as soon as I entered the house and now sat only a few feet from me, obviously worried. "But he saw those cards and kept picking them up and dropping them in here."

"It's okay," I said. "It's not like they're family heirlooms or anything."

No, they were just a regular pack of plain vanilla Rider-Waite cards.

"He seemed awfully excited," Lexi put in. "Once he had them all in the living room, he kept scooting them around as if he wanted them in a particular order."

A particular order? Was he trying to communicate via the Tarot cards, since he'd decided I was useless with the rune stones?

Edgar was sitting on the couch, a card in his beak. As I approached, he let go, and it fluttered to the floor.

Just as I was bending down to pick it up, my phone rang from inside my purse. A glance toward the rug told me the card had landed face down, so I couldn't tell what it was.

Well, it wasn't going anywhere.

I pulled out my cell phone and looked down at the screen.

Noah's number.

Hand shaking, I touched the screen to accept the call, then lifted it to my ear.

"H-hello?"

His voice, familiar, reassuring, despite everything that had passed between us.

"Hi, Charity.

"I think we need to talk."

Chapter 15

Queen for a Day

Even though this was spectacularly bad timing, I wasn't about to tell Noah that. "'Talk'?" I echoed. "Um, sure. When?"

"How about now? I can come over to your place."

Under other circumstances, I would have been thrilled by such an offer. Now, though, as I looked at the Tarot cards strewn all over my living room, I could only hope that I'd be able to get things reasonably tidied up before he appeared.

"Sure," I said, even as I bent down to pick up the card Edgar had dropped on the rug.

The Queen of Cups, blonde and serene on her throne. Well, I'd worry about her later.

"Then I'll be there in about fifteen minutes."

Fifteen minutes. I could manage that. Sure, I was probably focusing on cleaning up the mess because that kept me from having to analyze my feelings about Noah calling me out of the blue, but my tidy Virgo self wouldn't allow him to walk into a disaster zone.

"Sounds great," I told him. "I'll see you soon."

We ended the call there, and I immediately looked over at Edgar. "I need to get this cleaned up. A friend of mine is coming over."

He spread his wings and croaked. A raven couldn't really shake his head, but I could tell he wasn't too thrilled with me right then.

"Who's coming over?" Milo demanded, and I got the feeling he was worried it might be Malcolm.

"Noah," I said shortly, and at once both dogs' tails began to wag.

"Noah's coming to the house?" Lexi asked, wispy ears perking up.

"Yes, and I need to get this place cleaned up!"

I shoved the Queen of Cups card into my purse, figuring I'd add it to the rest of the deck when I had a chance. But even as I began walking purposefully toward the other cards where they lay on the floor, Edgar swooped in and grabbed one in his beak and another pair in his talons.

"Hey!" I exclaimed. "I'm trying to clean up this mess!"

He couldn't croak at me, not with his beak full like that, but he flew out of the room and down the hall to the office, and then came back to grab another couple of cards. Once he was done with that, he seemed much calmer, and even landed on the back of the sofa and watched with some interest as I scurried around, gathering the rest of the scattered deck, plumping cushions, picking up the water glass I'd left sitting on the coffee table since the day before.

Not a moment too soon, because a knock came at the front door just as I was slipping the cards into one of the coffee table's drawers.

"Outside," I told the dogs.

"But we want to see Noah," Milo said, and I bent down to ruffle his ears.

"I know you do, kiddo," I replied. "But this is a conversation I need to have without an audience, okay?"

To my surprise, Lexi was the one who saved me. "Some things need to be private," she said, looking straight at Milo. "We don't mind going outside, do we? And you, too, Edgar," she added, with a stern glance at the raven.

He seemed to realize he needed to listen to the diminutive dog, because he didn't croak in protest but only flew off toward the kitchen, presumably so the dogs could help him get through the doggy door there.

Left blessedly alone, I reached up to smooth my unruly hair as best I could—thank God I'd washed it this morning and had even put on a little makeup—and then headed for the front door.

Noah stood outside, looking diffident. He wore a barn jacket over a green sweater and jeans, and once again I was struck by how casually gorgeous he was. "I hope I didn't interrupt anything."

"Oh, no," I said hurriedly. "You know how it is here on Sundays—I'm just catching up on house stuff. Come on in."

I stepped out of the way so he could enter the living room. As he did so, I sent a worried look up toward the sky. It didn't seem as though it was going to start raining yet, and I prayed it would hold off for a while. I didn't want to cast another rain-delay spell...but I also knew I couldn't in good conscience force the animals to stay outside if it truly started to come down.

"Do you want anything?" I asked Noah. "Some water, or tea?"

Or a big glass of wine, I added mentally, although I guessed I probably shouldn't say that out loud.

"Water is fine," he replied, as though glad I'd come up with a way to delay the really serious stuff for a few minutes more.

Because that had to be why he'd come over here, didn't it? Otherwise, there would have been no reason for us to talk in person.

Or maybe I was only thinking that because it was what I desperately wanted to believe.

"Great," I said. "Go ahead and sit down—I'll be back in a minute."

He went over to the couch and took a seat somewhere in the middle, while I hurried into the kitchen and poured us two glasses of water from the pitcher in the fridge. My hands shook a little, and I told them to get it together. The last thing I wanted was for him to see how much his coming over today had shaken me.

Then again, being Noah, he'd probably already noticed that his arrival had thrown me way off balance.

But I made myself take a few breaths, then picked up the glasses of water and went back into the living room. Since he'd sat down toward the middle of the couch, I seated myself a little ways away as I handed one glass to him.

"Thanks," he said, then took a sip. I couldn't say for sure whether he was actually thirsty, or whether he'd drunk the water because, now that he was sitting here next to me, he wasn't quite sure how to begin.

I drank as well. It was harder than I'd thought it would be to have him so close, to feel how real he was, from the tousle of brown hair that waved so perfectly back from his brow to the strength of the tanned fingers wrapped around the glass he held.

But I knew I needed to act calm. Not entirely cool, because the last thing I wanted was for him to think I was indifferent, and yet at the same time, I didn't want to give the impression that I was ready to lay into him for the way we'd split up.

He set his glass of water down on a coaster, then shifted on the sofa so he almost—but not quite—faced me. Those bright blue eyes were unflinching as he said, "I've been a complete jackass."

That was the last thing I'd expected to hear. "Noah—" I began, but he shook his head.

"No, I was. I knew that you'd kept this whole witch thing from me because it was necessary. More than necessary—absolutely vital, not to mention something that your people have been doing for generations. I got so hung up on the way you'd kept secrets from me without letting myself really stop and think hard about why you'd done it."

"It's okay," I said. "I mean, it was kind of a lot. And I really did want to tell you, only…."

"Only you had to be sure of me first," he replied. His hand shifted where it rested on his knee, and I wondered if he'd started to reach out to me but hadn't quite found the courage.

I wasn't feeling overly courageous right then, either—mostly hopeful and worried at the same time—but I still made myself reach out and touch his hand. Briefly, barely a brush of my fingers against his, and yet I still prayed it would be enough to get the message across.

"Yes, I did," I said. "I think I knew deep down how right we were for each other, but I've never been the sort of person to make the first move when it comes to that kind of thing."

"And I should've said something." He stopped there, and now he did reach over and take my hand, gently, and yet I could still feel the strength of his fingers, how I somehow knew he wouldn't let go unless I did so first. "Maybe I was gun-shy after that whole thing with Shelby. I don't know. That was stupid, though—you're nothing like her. I knew things would be different with you."

There was an understatement. His former fiancée had broken off their engagement when he made it clear that he didn't want to stay in the big city any longer, while she wanted to remain in Boston and enjoy the kind of lifestyle that generations of wealth had provided for her.

"Still, it's understandable," I said. "I get it, I really do. I just wish you'd talked about it more."

Noah's mouth twisted in something that was halfway between a grimace and a smile. "The guys in my family don't talk about that kind of stuff. Football scores and fishing trips and home improvement, sure."

"Well, you needed to talk to me," I said firmly.

"I would have understood. And I also understand that what I dumped on you was a lot for anyone to handle." I hesitated, wondering whether I should dance around the issue a bit longer, or whether I should cut straight through to the heart of the matter. "I guess my question is, are you okay with this whole witch thing? I mean, if you're not, I totally understand. We can still be friendly—"

I didn't get any further than that, though, because Noah leaned in and pressed his mouth against mine, letting me know in no uncertain terms that he was just fine with me being a witch. Happy tingles went all through me, reminding me of what I'd already known—that he was the only man I would ever truly love, and no one else could ever hope to take his place. When he pulled away afterward, though, his eyes were still worried.

"Was that all right? I don't want you to think I was forcing you into something you didn't want."

At once, I took both his hands in mine. "That was more than all right," I told him. "Don't you think I've been hoping for this moment for the past month?"

Now the smile he wore was genuine. "I didn't want to presume anything."

"You aren't." Still holding his hands, I looked up into his face, into those blue eyes that were a promise of bright summers yet to come. "So...does this mean we're back together?"

He didn't blink. "If you'll have me."

Oh, I'll have you six ways from Sunday, I thought. "I thought it was pretty obvious that I wanted you back."

"Well, then," he said. "I just want to put all this past us." He stopped there, his expression darkening somewhat. "What about that guy?"

"What guy?"

"The one you were with at the Halloween ball."

Honestly, Malcolm Grimes had so utterly vanished from my thoughts, it was almost as if he didn't exist at all. "What about him?" I returned. "We went out that one time. And I promise you, there was zero chemistry. I knew I wouldn't go out with him again."

The set of Noah's shoulders relaxed, and he smiled. "Okay. That's good news. I told myself I shouldn't be angry that you'd moved on, especially after the way I've acted around you, but when I saw you with that guy—"

I remembered my wistful fancies from the ball, how I'd desperately hoped Noah would be stricken by jealousy as soon as he saw me with Malcolm. Kind of funny to think those hopes and wishes had come true.

"So...you were jealous?" I asked, only half teasing.

"Eaten up by it," Noah said cheerfully. "And I

went home last night and did some hard thinking. I had to admit to myself that I wouldn't have felt that way if I was truly over you, and if I still had feelings for you, I'd better come over here and properly grovel and see if you'd take me back."

"The groveling definitely worked," I replied with a grin, and he leaned in and kissed me again, the kind of kiss that proved once and for all that Noah Jenkins was the only man in the world for me.

His expression turned serious. "Then I want to tell you what I should have told you months ago. I love you, Charity Hughes, and I want to be a part of your life."

He'd said it. A rush of warmth went through me, not desire exactly, although that was mixed in as well. No, it was more like those three small words had made real all the hopes and fears of the past four months.

Noah Jenkins loved me.

And that meant I needed to let him know how I felt as well.

"I love you, Noah," I said. "Honestly, I think I've been in love with you since the moment I set foot in your office that first time over a year ago."

Another kiss, another perfect moment while he held me in his arms and I knew nothing in the world could be any better than this.

All right, maybe one thing might be a *teensy* bit better than his kisses.

When we broke apart this time, though, I realized that Milo and Lexi and Edgar were still outside, and the day kept getting darker and darker, promising some real weather.

"I need to let the dogs in," I said, hoping Noah could hear the apologetic note in my voice. "They're out there with my latest familiar project, Edgar."

"Who's Edgar?" Noah asked, now looking amused.

"A raven," I replied as I got up from the couch.

"Of course he is."

Pretty much the same thing I'd thought when Sally first dropped off her familiar, proving once again that Noah and I were sympatico in a way I couldn't fully explain.

I paused to brush a kiss against his hair, then hurried to the back door. The first drops of rain had just begun to fall as I opened it, and Milo and Lexi rushed in, followed by Edgar, who'd been perched in the oak tree and watching to see when I would emerge.

"How is Noah?" Milo asked, and I smiled.

"He's fine. We're fine."

Both dogs stared at me. Edgar, who'd landed on the back of one of the kitchen chairs, didn't look quite so interested, but I could understand that. He'd never met the man, hadn't understood there'd been a big chunk of my life missing when Sally Hawkins dropped her raven off a few days earlier.

"Does that mean...?" Milo began. His tail had already begun to wag, but I could tell from the hesitation in his voice that he wasn't quite sure whether he could allow himself to hope that Noah and I had reconciled.

"Yes, we're back together. So go on in there and say hi."

Both dogs rushed out of the kitchen and into the living room, while Edgar flew up from the chair and landed on my shoulder. I didn't know for sure what that meant, although I guessed he wanted to be close to me when I made the introductions.

Noah had gotten up when I came back in, Lexi and Milo standing with their forepaws placed on his legs so he could more easily bend down and scratch their ears and pet them and generally give them all the love they'd been missing from him during the past month. However, as I entered he straightened, gaze going immediately to the raven perched on my shoulder.

"Edgar, I presume."

"Yes," I said. "His mistress brought him over a couple of days ago."

"He looks healthy enough," Noah observed as

he looked the bird over with his keen veterinarian's eyes.

"Oh, there's hardly ever something physically wrong with a familiar when a witch brings them over for me to help with them," I replied. "It's usually that there's a misunderstanding, some kind of friction. My job is to figure out the root cause and try to work it out so they can continue to get along in the future."

"Kind of like a pet therapist," he said.

"Sort of." It was actually a bit more complicated than that, but I didn't see any reason to get into the minutiae right now.

"So, what kind of problem was he having?" Noah asked before adding quickly, "If you have some kind of patient-client privilege, I understand why you might not be able to talk about it."

"Nothing like that," I assured him, now a little amused. "I guess about a week ago, Edgar stopped talking to his mistress and instead started communicating with rune stones."

"'Rune stones'?" Noah repeated, expression puzzled.

I wasn't too surprised that he'd never heard of them. It wasn't as if he'd been steeped in arcana from almost the day he was born.

"They're a form of divination. Each set of rune stones has twenty-four stones, each one carved with a different rune based on the ancient Norse alphabet, and each with its own meaning. Some people prefer them to the Tarot or other means of telling the future. Anyway, Sally cast a spell on him make him use runes to communicate rather than talk to her, mostly so she'd have a reason to drop him off here while she went vacationing in Cape Cod with her boyfriend." I stopped there, smiling a little at Noah's startled expression. It was kind of a crazy story when you made yourself really consider it. But then I went on, "Each stone can have a lot of different interpretations, so it's been tough to figure out what he's really trying to say."

Noah shook his head. "I can imagine."

"But I guess he decided I was too clueless to deal with the rune stones, so right before you came over, he took my Tarot cards and threw them all over the place."

"I don't see how that could be helpful."

I hadn't, either, although....

"When I was tidying up, he grabbed five of the cards and took them into my office," I said. "Maybe there's something significant about those...and the Queen of Cups."

"The Queen of Cups?" Noah responded, now looking completely mystified.

"That card was lying on the floor when I came in," I explained. "I shoved it in my purse. Let me get it, and then we can go look at the other cards he pulled."

Was that a flicker of disappointment in Noah's eyes? I supposed I could understand that—we'd kissed and made up, but it would have been nice to go upstairs to my bedroom and really seal the deal —and yet, once again the witch world had interfered.

Well, he'd have to get used to it. Working with familiars was part of who I was, and I needed to do my best to figure out what Edgar had been attempting to tell me.

I'd be sure to make it up to Noah later.

He seemed game enough as we all went into my office, though, with Lexi and Milo trotting at our heels and Edgar still riding on my shoulder. It was a small space originally intended as a ground-floor bedroom, but I needed an office a lot more than I needed a place for guests to stay. That was why it had a small desk and a pair of bookcases, along with a shabby leather office chair my mother had given me when she deemed it not Instagram-worthy any longer.

Lying on the desktop were the five cards Edgar had retrieved from the rest of the pile and brought here. Two were face up, and three lay face down. I turned over those three and saw that he'd fetched the Two card from each suit: Two of Pentacles, Two of Cups, Two of Wands, Two of Swords.

Why those cards? They had wildly divergent meanings because they came from four different suits. Was there some other symbology going on here that I hadn't yet puzzled out?

The fifth card was the Magician. In silence, I pulled the Queen of Cups from my purse and laid it on the desktop next to the other cards.

Edgar immediately launched himself from my shoulder and landed on the desk, then nudged the Queen card a little closer to the Magician.

"What does it mean?" Noah asked in a murmur, as though he was worried that if he raised his voice, he might upset the raven.

"I have absolutely no idea," I said. "All those twos? They mean something very different from one another. It's not like it's a four-of-a-kind like we're playing poker or something."

He frowned and rubbed the stubble on his chin. I could tell he hadn't shaved this morning, and I was just fine with that. He was even more attractive—if possible—when he looked a little grungy.

"What about the Magician?"

Well, at least that part was a little more straight-forward. "Meanings can change a little when they're interpreted along with the other cards in a spread, but generally, the Magician is a positive card. It represents resourcefulness, forward motion. Well, as long as it isn't reversed."

Noah gave a very small nod. "And when it's reversed?"

"Manipulation, wasted resources." I frowned as I stared down at the cards. Edgar had jumbled them all together, so it was kind of hard to tell whether the Magician had been reversed or upright.

I thought of the cards I'd pulled this morning —the Tower, the Four of Pentacles reversed, the Ten of Swords. There had been a whole bunch of negativity in that reading, and I wondered if I could add manipulation to betrayal and all the others.

"What about the Queen of Cups?" Noah asked.

"She's also usually a positive card," I said. "But reversed, she can signify co-dependency." I released a breath, then added, "To be honest, none of this makes much sense. Maybe Edgar wasn't trying to communicate with the cards at all."

As soon as I uttered those words, though, he let out one of his hoarse croaks and pushed his beak against the Queen of Cups card, brown eyes pleading, as though he could somehow transmit what he was trying to tell me through mere thought alone.

It didn't work that way, though. At least, not with an animal who wasn't my familiar.

He looked back down at my desk. As usual, it was its regular messy jumble, with the Tarot cards lying on top of some bills that needed to be paid, along with the mail I'd brought in the day before—

a few advertising flyers, the latest batch of weekly specials from the local grocery stores.

Something he saw there got him excited, though, because he pushed and pulled at the sales flyers until one came out on top.

An ad for Jessica Owens' New Age shop, with a photo of her smiling broadly as she stood against a wall of shelves displaying various types of crystals.

Edgar tapped his beak against the photo of Jessica, and then went over and did the same thing with the Queen of Cups card.

Excitement stirred. "Are you trying to say you used that card to mean Jessica Owens?"

He hopped up and down, and croaked again.

"Why would he be talking about her?" Noah asked as he peered over my shoulder at the sales flyer. "She's the owner of that woo-woo shop down the street from your place, right?"

I had a feeling he'd never set foot in that store, so it didn't surprise me too much that he didn't know a lot about Jessica. "Yes, she is," I said. "But I'm not sure why Edgar would be so interested in her."

Apparently, the raven didn't much like that comment, because he tapped his beak against the picture of Jessica Owens once again before he hopped over to the Tarot cards and did the same thing with all of the Twos in their various suits.

"I'm not following," Noah remarked.

That made two of us...no pun intended. "I don't understand, Edgar," I said slowly, looking from Jessica's picture to the scattered set of Twos and back again. "Are you trying to tell us there are two Jessicas?"

Which made absolutely no sense.

Edgar didn't seem to think much of my theory, either, because he clicked his beak and then made an odd gesture with one foot, as though he was trying his best to point at himself.

Clear as mud.

Now obviously frustrated, the raven went to a different sales flyer and tugged away part of the paper, tearing off the letters "S-A-L." After that, he pulled out another flyer, this one from Redhawk Realty, and did the same thing, this time isolating "HAWK." He nudged the two pieces of paper together, then cocked a bright eye at me, something in his expression indicating that he thought I'd be an utter dunce if I didn't figure this one out.

Sal Hawk.

"Sally Hawkins?" I ventured, and Edgar croaked again, then pushed the Two of Cups toward the photo of Jessica Owens.

Oh, my God.

I looked up at Noah, who still looked supremely confused.

"Sally Hawkins is Edgar's mistress," I said.

"I think what he's trying to tell us is that she and Jessica Owens are sisters."

Chapter 16

Sold Sisters

Brows still pulled together in a frown, Noah said, "Does that mean Jessica Owens is a witch?"

"No, she's definitely a mundane," I replied, then added, "That's what witches call nonmagical people."

"Well, I guess it's better than 'muggle,'" Noah said with a grin.

Maybe so.

Before I could say anything, though, he continued. "Can a witch have a sister who isn't also a witch?"

"It happens from time to time," I said. "That's why a lot of witches stop after having one daughter—they don't want to take the risk that a second child might not inherit their magic. So it's not unprecedented, although it's fairly rare."

"So, how does that even work?"

Not very well, I thought. The witch world had a mechanism for dealing with these sorts of situations, but it wasn't an elegant one.

"Our powers start to show up fairly early," I explained. "If they don't, then usually we'll try to find a distant relative who also was born without powers to take the girl and raise her. But if there aren't relatives, then those children are either fostered or adopted."

"That's kind of cold," Noah said. His expression wasn't exactly disapproving, but I could tell he thought having someone else raise a witch without powers was kind of the nuclear option.

"I've always been told it's best for everyone," I said.

"But you don't believe it."

This really wasn't the time for a discussion about what I might or might not believe. "I'm lucky enough that it's never been an issue in my family. The magic has come down from generation to generation without a single daughter being born without powers. And I have no idea what happened with Sally and Jessica, because they're from a different town and a different coven—at least, Sally's from that coven. But even if they were raised apart, it seems like they must have known they were sisters, or Edgar here wouldn't have been working so hard to connect the dots."

The raven tapped his beak against the photo of Jessica Owens, and I regarded him thoughtfully.

"There's something else you're trying to tell us, though?" I asked, and he flapped his wings.

"It looks like you're communicating just fine," Noah said, blue eyes crinkling at the corners in amusement.

"We are now," I replied. "This felt harder a couple of days ago."

Maybe it had been. After all, Sally herself had admitted that she'd placed a spell on the raven to force him to use the rune stones to communicate, so it made sense that maybe the enchantment had started to wear off, to weaken over time.

I looked back over at Edgar. "This is about more than just Sally and Jessica, isn't it?"

The raven let out another of those harsh croaks. Milo and Lexi had been sitting near the corner, obviously doing their best to stay out of the way, but my cocker spaniel seemed compelled to speak up now.

"He got more agitated after he heard Sally was coming to get him tomorrow," Milo told me. "I don't think he wants to go."

"Or maybe he's just distressed about going home without me figuring out what was going on with him," I said.

Edgar tapped the table with his beak. Did that mean he agreed with one of us, or neither?

Before I could ask any other questions, the doorbell rang. Noah looked over at me, eyebrows raised.

"Were you expecting someone?"

"No," I said, equally puzzled. "Everyone knows to call before they drop by, because of the way I have so many fosters coming in and out of here."

"Election canvassers," he suggested.

I supposed that was remotely possible—we were having a municipal election on Tuesday—but I'd never had anyone bother to stop by before this. The houses in this neighborhood were spread too far apart to make that kind of activity worth anyone's while.

The doorbell rang again, and I sighed. "Well, I'd better see who it is. You can hang out here while I get rid of them."

Noah nodded, and I headed out of the office and through the living room. When I opened the front door, my mouth sagged slightly in shock.

Malcolm Grimes stood on the front step, looking much different from the previous evening, since he now wore a leather jacket over a dark red sweater and jeans. Rain had started to come down in earnest, leaving wet splotches on the shoulders of his jacket.

"Sorry to drop in like this," he said. "But it turned out I needed to come back up to Salem to handle some business, so I thought I'd swing by and get the dress from you while I was here."

"Oh, sure," I said, and stepped out of the way. "Come on in."

And thank God Noah and the animals were all in the office. With any luck, I could get rid of Malcolm quickly and he'd never even have to know I'd had other company.

Well, except for Noah's truck. However, he'd parked on the street and not in the driveway, so it still wasn't completely obvious that the owner of the vehicle was at my house and not someone else's.

"The dress is hanging up in my bedroom closet," I went on. "Just give me a minute to go upstairs and grab it."

"Of course."

Nothing in his expression told me he was disappointed that I hadn't offered him something to drink or even asked him to sit down, which was a relief. I just wanted to hand over the dress and get him out of there so Noah and I could go back to talking to Edgar and trying to figure out what he was trying to communicate.

I hurried up the stairs and went immediately to the closet, glad I'd had the presence of mind to hang up the costume's various parts the night before and put the garment bag over the entire ensemble. That meant I could grab it and run back down to the living room...only to see a black blur come flying out of the office and launch itself at Malcolm's head.

"Ow!" he yelled, throwing himself to the floor and missing Edgar's attack by less than an inch.

"What the hell, Edgar?" I shouted. "You come right back here!"

But I wasn't his mistress, and that meant he didn't need to obey my commands. Instead, he flew at Malcolm again, talons outstretched.

Another blur, only this one was Noah, who made an absolutely superb flying tackle and managed to grab the ferocious raven before he could take a chunk out of Malcolm's ear. True, he didn't quite stick the landing, and slid across the rug before smacking into a side table and knocking over the lamp that sat there.

Luckily, it had a metal base, so it didn't break when it fell, although the shade looked like it was a goner.

Edgar was writhing in Noah's arms, but since my boyfriend had years of experience dealing with squirmy animals, he wasn't getting away. In the meantime, Malcolm had managed to push himself to his feet and was now glaring at the raven.

"What is that creature doing here?"

"I'm raven-sitting," I said blithely. Ravens didn't attack like that out of the blue, so I had to assume the two were previously acquainted. "You know each other, don't you?"

Malcolm's eyes narrowed. I couldn't help noticing the way he was pointedly ignoring Noah's presence, which was fine by me.

I wasn't in the mood to make introductions, anyway.

"I've never seen that bird before in my life."

Edgar croaked, only this time, it wasn't just a guttural noise.

No, it sounded almost like "liar."

Malcolm's jaw set, but instead of acknowledging Edgar's editorial comment, he only plucked the gown from my arms, saying, "It seems you have your hands full right now. I'll call you later."

I almost said, *Don't bother,* but decided to let it go.

I could always block his number.

He stalked out of the living room, then slammed the front door a moment later. I looked over at Noah, and he let go of Edgar, who fluttered away so he could land on my shoulder.

"Where did you see Malcolm before?" I asked.

Another croak, one that sounded remarkably like, "Home."

Okay, then.

It looked like we were about to take a field trip to Middleton.

Noah insisted on coming—not that I would have tried to stop him. Since I still didn't know exactly what I was dealing with here, it just seemed better to have some backup. And although Sally had told me she wouldn't be home until tomorrow, some witchy sixth sense told me the whole story about Cape Cod and the man named Hank had been a complete lie, and she'd been at her house the whole time.

I rode with Edgar in the passenger seat of Noah's pickup truck, since he'd offered to drive. The rain was really coming down now, rippling across the road in sheets.

Well, I supposed it could have been worse. At least the temperatures weren't cold enough yet for it to turn to sleet or snow.

And it seemed as if everyone had decided this was a good day to stay inside and catch up on their reading, because the roads, if not deserted, definitely weren't very busy. We made good time, even with Noah watching his speed, thanks to the slippery asphalt.

"Sally's house is on Fairway Drive," I said after we crossed over Middleton's town limits. Thank goodness I always got their full contact information from my clients, just in case of an emergency.

Noah dutifully turned left onto the street in question, and soon enough, we were pulling up in front of her house, a pale green split-level that looked as though it had been built sometime in the late forties or early fifties.

And thank goodness that I immediately spied a vaguely familiar white Subaru, still with its dealer plates, parked in the driveway. It looked as though Sally Hawkins was back from her trip to Cape Cod, which made some sense, considering it was Sunday and she probably had chores to deal with before she started back with her normal work schedule the next day.

If, of course, she'd even been gone at all, which I was doubting more and more.

Noah and I had both donned jackets before we left my house, so I pulled up my hood to protect my hair from the rain, which was coming down harder than ever. I had Edgar snuggled inside my coat, and he was safe and dry.

Even with the hood, I knew my hair was going to turn into a wavy, frizzy mass. But since Noah had already seen me at my worst and loved me anyway, I wasn't going to worry about it.

No, we marched up the trio of steps that led to Sally Hawkins' red-painted front door, and Noah knocked while I waited next to him.

A moment later, Sally opened the door and

stared out at me, mystified. "I thought I was picking Edgar up tomorrow," she ventured, her words ending on an upward inflection, almost but not quite a question.

"You were," I said calmly. "But something came up, and we thought we'd better talk to you."

"'We'?" she repeated, sending a doubtful look at Noah.

"We," I said, my tone firm. "Can we come in? It's pouring out here."

Courtesy must have overcome doubt, because she stepped out of the way so we could enter the small foyer. Because the house was a split-level, a short staircase behind her looked as though it led up to the living areas, while a second one off to our left appeared to go to the lower level, maybe a rumpus room or some bedrooms.

"We can sit down in the living room," she said as Noah and I tagged along behind her. "Do you want any tea or coffee? It's such a cold, dreary day."

While under other circumstances, I might have taken her up on her offer, now I didn't want any delays in getting to the heart of the reason why we were here. And a small head shake from Noah told me he was thinking the same thing.

"No, we're fine," I replied, and unbuttoned my coat so Edgar could peek out.

Once he saw he was in familiar surroundings, he immediately freed himself the rest of the way and went to sit on a perch that it seemed Sally had made for him especially, an interesting piece constructed of gnarled oak branches that was definitely at odds with the beige, nondescript decor in the rest of the room.

After Noah and I had seated ourselves on the sofa and Sally had sat down on one of the accent chairs that faced it, she sent us a curious look. "What's this about?"

"We know that you and Jessica Owens are sisters," I said bluntly, and at once, the small bit of color in Sally's cheeks faded.

However, her physical reaction to my statement didn't seem to prevent her from protesting, "Jessica who? I don't know what you're talking about—I don't have a sister."

"Yes, you do," I said, not caring much how brusque I sounded. "Edgar told us. She was born without magic, right?"

Sally looked around the room, almost as if she was hoping to find something there that would offer her salvation. But because it was empty except for the furniture and a few knickknacks that I guessed were nonmagical in nature, I doubted she would locate anything that might help her.

"I don't have a sister," she said again, as if she thought that if she repeated the words enough times, they would suddenly come true.

"We know you do," Noah said, his voice a lot

gentler than mine. "And we know you were working with Malcolm Grimes somehow—Edgar had a violent reaction to the man when he showed up at Charity's house a little while ago. So why don't you tell us what's really going on?"

"If you've gotten tangled up in something that's gone beyond your control, it's better to come clean," I chimed in, doing my best to sound as friendly, as nonjudgmental as Noah. Whether I was successful or not was up for debate, but Sally seemed to sag then, as though she'd realized her protests of innocence weren't going to get her anywhere.

"Yes, Jessica is my sister," she said, voice a low monotone, as if she thought reciting the facts in such an unemotional way might make it easier to face up to the situation. "I knew she existed, obviously, since she's three years younger than I am, but she was sent away when she was very young, not much more than four. My mother kept in touch with her adoptive mother, since she was another magicless witch, but it sounded as if Jessica didn't remember anything about her early days or her life here in Middleton."

"She must have remembered something, or you wouldn't have met," Noah observed dryly, and Sally's mouth pursed.

"No, what happened was that when her adoptive mother was on her deathbed, she confessed everything. Jessica came and confronted me, and I told her that yes, she was my younger sister, but because she didn't have any magic, she couldn't be a part of my life."

That must have gone over well. I didn't say anything, only kept my gaze fixed on the older woman, waiting for her to go on.

"She took it better than I expected," Sally continued. "But she stayed in the area—moved to Salem and bought a shop with her inheritance, and it seemed as if she was content with her life."

I wasn't so sure about that. It seemed to me that Jessica had done everything she could to make people think she was a witch—owning a New Age store, sashaying around town in outfits that wouldn't have been out of place in a Pyramid Collection catalog. And of course most people believed her witchy act, because Salem was full of people pretending to be witches who really weren't.

"Something changed, though, didn't it?" I ventured, and again Sally's mouth tightened.

"Yes. A while back, Jessica came to me all excited because she'd read how Malcolm Grimes was offering $500,000 to anyone who could provide him with hard evidence that witches existed. She told me I could go to him and do some magic, and that we'd split the money."

Half a million dollars was a lot of money. It

wouldn't be enough for me to betray the witch community, but I could see how it might be tempting for someone who seemed to live a very modest existence...despite the brand-new car in the driveway.

"You took him up on the offer?" Noah asked. His tone was almost too neutral, telling me he didn't think much of someone who was willing to sell out their people for a few bucks.

Sally's hands knotted on her knees. Her thin fingers were bare of rings, and she kept her nails short and unpolished.

Not the sort of person who would probably blow through $250,000 right away.

"I was reluctant at first," Sally replied. "But Jessica kept working on me, and I finally gave in." A pause, and she burst out, "What difference did it make? I've always been a mediocre witch—that's why my spell on Edgar wore off so fast. I figured I'd get something out of being a witch besides a life alone, one where I had to hide who I was from almost everyone."

"It was wrong to do that to your familiar," I said, choosing to ignore the rest of her comment. I'd be the first to admit that sometimes being a witch felt like a raw deal—having to conceal a huge part of your nature from almost everyone, often having to spend your life on your own if you weren't lucky enough to find a soul mate—but all the same, I would never betray the witch community the way Sally had tried to do.

"Edgar is a very smart bird," she said, and the raven ruffled his feathers before settling back down on his perch. "It wasn't just that he and I could communicate the way a familiar and a witch always do. He could croak a few words and could read enough that he would also be able to spell out a brief message. There was always a chance he might say something to the other members of my coven, and I couldn't let that happen."

"So you put the spell on him about the rune stones so you could have me try to work with him?" I asked, and she nodded.

"That wasn't my plan at first. But even after I placed the enchantment on him, Jessica started obsessing over the possibility that he might still say something to someone. I was worried about him, and I thought he'd be safer with you."

Noah's brows drew together. "You thought Jessica might harm your raven?"

Now looking miserable, Sally nodded again. "I didn't want to believe that about her," she said, her voice now barely more than a murmur. "I didn't want to think she was capable of violence. But she has a terrible temper, and after a lifetime of being lied to, she isn't about to let anything stand in her way."

And that was where it fell into place...even if I

didn't have all the facts yet. "Jessica is the one who killed Eunice Bartlett with that hunk of pyrite."

Sally pulled in a breath, gaze seemingly fixed on the rug beneath her feet so she wouldn't have to look at any of us. "I think so," she said, still in that low, fast tone. "She never came out and confessed to me, but she told me last week that I needed to hurry up and arrange a meeting with Malcolm Grimes because she'd heard that Dr. Bartlett was already claiming to have incontrovertible proof that witches existed."

"What proof was that?" Noah asked, and Sally's thin shoulders lifted.

"I don't know. Whatever it was, her secret must have died with her. All I know is that Jessica was worried Dr. Bartlett would scoop us, for lack of a better term. And if she got her findings out in the world before Malcolm Grimes did, then we wouldn't get the reward he was offering."

A heavy silence fell then, and Noah shot me a significant glance from under his thick brown eyelashes. Was he thinking the same thing I was?

Only one way to find out.

"Does Malcolm Grimes know that Jessica killed Eunice to get her out of the way?"

Another lift of her shoulders, one that wasn't so much careless as utterly unsure. "I don't know. I haven't talked to him recently—Jessica was the one who always met with him." A pause, and then she said, expression now almost disapproving, "I think she has kind of a crush on him. It was always 'Malcolm this' and 'Malcolm that.' She didn't really talk about it, but I think she kept hoping that he'd be interested in her and whisk her away to a life of luxury or something."

No wonder Jessica had come storming into my shop the way she had, doing her best to warn me off from her object of desire. I wasn't interested in Malcolm that way, but she didn't know that. And as someone younger than her and an actual witch —at least, I assumed she knew what I was, considering how Sally had spilled the beans about so many other things—I supposed in Jessica's mind, I would have constituted a real threat.

Malcolm was definitely the wild card in the situation. Had he come to see me because he'd known Jessica was the killer, and had wanted to retrieve whatever evidence he could find so it wouldn't incriminate her? That would make him an accessory after the fact, wouldn't it?

I didn't know for sure. While I might have solved a few murders, I certainly wasn't an expert on the law.

"And what about Trent Abernathy?" I asked then. "One of you planted the evidence in his store, didn't you?"

Now Sally looked so miserable, I wasn't sure whether she was about to start crying. Her eyes were suspiciously bright, but she managed to hold it together as she said, again in that whispery murmur, "I did that. It was Jessica's idea, but I'm the one who magicked the stone into his store and made sure there was no physical evidence from Jessica on it."

"You were okay with framing an innocent man?" Noah asked, his voice hard.

"I wasn't okay!" Sally burst out, and then knotted her hands in her lap as though ashamed of the way she'd lost control, if even for just a moment. "But Jessica said she was pretty sure a jury would decide in the end that there wasn't enough evidence and that Trent would go free eventually."

"After being put through the stress of a murder trial," I said, my tone just as cold as Noah's. "And maybe losing his business to pay for his legal costs. Did you ever think about that?"

She shook her head. "No. It's just...by then, I was trapped in this whole thing. I just wanted to do whatever I had to so I could make it go away. Can't you understand that?"

No, I really couldn't, mostly because I would never have allowed myself to be trapped in such a terrible situation.

The problem was, I couldn't report Sally to the authorities. Whatever else she'd done, she was still a witch—if not a very good one—and that meant it was up to her coven to deal with her.

Jessica, on the other hand....

"I've heard enough," I said, rising from my seat on the couch while Noah did the same.

"What are you going to do?" Sally asked, real fear in her voice.

"Whatever I have to," I replied.

Chapter 17

A House by the Sea

Noah drove, and I called Ruth McCoy, the woman I knew was the nominal head of the Middleton witches. We weren't terribly well-acquainted, but all the covens in the area maintained at least one point of contact in each group so we'd have someone to reach out to if a problem arose.

And a problem had definitely arisen here.

She listened to my story in growing horror, and at the end, she told me that she and the other members of her coven would handle it.

What that meant exactly, I wasn't sure, but at least Sally Hawkins was now someone else's problem.

"Are you really going to confront Jessica?" Noah asked after we'd driven for a few more minutes. The rain had let up a little, but it was still coming down hard enough that he didn't dare take his eyes off the road.

"I might—if I even knew where to find her. It's Sunday, and that means her shop is closed. And while I know she lives in Salem, I have no idea where. I actually have something better in mind."

His eyebrow lifted. "What's that?"

So I explained my plan to him, and he nodded in grim satisfaction. "Turnabout. I like it."

That was why, when we got to Salem, we went to my mother's house rather than heading straight home. As briefly as I could, I filled her in on what had been happening with Sally Hawkins and her long-lost sister.

"But I'll need the whole coven for this," I concluded. "It's kind of a tricky piece of magic."

"Not a problem," she replied. "Since it's Sunday and the weather isn't so great, I'm sure everyone is available."

Which turned out to be the case. The coven gathered in my mother's basement, and Noah waited upstairs in the living room while we all cast the necessary spell.

One final bit, though. I got out my cell phone and called the Salem police department—making sure my caller ID was blocked—and then told the startled deputy at the other end of the line that they might like to recheck the hunk of pyrite they'd found at Trent Abernathy's shop, and that what they found would prove he had nothing to do with Eunice Bartlett's murder.

"And now we wait," I said as I ended the call.

"Hopefully, not for very long," my mother said, and the other members of the coven nodded their agreement.

"What about this Malcolm Grimes person?" Grace Bowersby asked. "He doesn't sound like a very savory character."

"I'm not totally sure," I said. "What Sally Hawkins told us doesn't seem to incriminate him one way or another...except for being willing to spend a whole lot of cash to prove witches exist. Still, there's nothing inherently illegal about that."

Although everyone gathered in the basement looked disapproving, no one spoke up to disagree with me. As much as we didn't like the idea, it wasn't against the law to leverage large sums of money to prove a pet theory.

The meeting broke up after that, and Noah and I finally headed for home—but not before my mother raised an eyebrow at the way we left together, telling me she was probably going to call sooner rather than later to find out just what was going on with the two of us.

Which was fine. To be honest, I wanted to shout from the rooftops that Noah and I were back together, but I'd settle for letting the Salem witch network do the heavy lifting of spreading that particular piece of news.

When we got home, the dogs were ecstatic to see us—even as Milo, after sniffing at our damp pant legs, sat down and sent us a quizzical look.

"What happened to Edgar?"

At once, I bent down to scratch behind his ears. "We left him at his house with Sally. Since we'd figured out what was going on with him, there wasn't any more reason for him to stay."

Once again, I couldn't help feeling guilty about the way we'd had to leave him behind in Middleton. But it wasn't as if I was the witch judge and jury—I couldn't take someone's familiar away from her just because I didn't like the way she'd behaved. That was up to the Middleton coven.

And besides, I couldn't take in every stray animal or familiar in the world. My little house was already feeling a bit tight with two dogs in it.

"Well, I'm glad you figured it out," Milo said. "Even if I get the feeling you aren't telling me everything."

No, I wasn't. At some point, I would explain to the dogs what exactly had happened with Edgar, but I didn't want to do so until the story had a true ending.

Instead, I took off my damp jacket while Noah did the same, and then went to the kitchen so I could give Lexi and Milo some treats for being such good doggies while we were away.

"You were talking to him, weren't you?" Noah asked as the two of them munched on their treats.

"I was," I said. "Is that weird to you?"

He grinned. "It might take some getting used to. You sound normal enough, but Milo's words just come out as growls and woofs and other dog noises."

"That's part of my gift," I said. "I can talk to any animal that's a familiar. Lexi's a slightly different case—her master definitely wasn't a witch, but she has a spell cast on her that allows her to talk to witches, so for all intents and purposes, it's about the same thing."

For a few seconds, Noah didn't say anything, and only watched the two dogs. "I've always wanted to be able to talk to animals," he commented after a moment. "So I think it's pretty cool that the woman I love can do that very thing."

He bent and kissed me then, and I let myself melt into his embrace. A small thing, maybe, but it was what I needed right then.

As for the rest...well, I just had to hope that the ball my coven and I had set in motion was about to roll down a *very* steep hill.

It seemed it had, because Derek called me the next morning. Noah had stayed over, of course, but he hadn't been able to linger because he needed to get to work. But since I had Mondays off, I was able to be a bit more of a sloth.

"We got an interesting tip yesterday," Derek said. "So we retested the evidence from Eunice Bartlett's murder. Turns out it wasn't Trent Abernathy's DNA on it at all."

"It wasn't?" I responded, hoping I sounded properly astonished.

"No," he said. "The DNA belonged to a woman named Jessica Owens. Her shop is just down the street from yours."

"So...*she's* the one who killed Dr. Bartlett?"

"It looks that way," Derek said, his tone now grim. "I have no idea how the lab messed up its testing so badly, but we brought her in for questioning and got a second sample, one that definitely proves she was the one who'd handled that rock. At first, she denied everything, but we've got her locked up for now...especially since we got some corroborating evidence from Malcolm Grimes that she would have had a clear motive."

"'Malcolm'?" I repeated, and didn't even have to try to sound startled that time.

"Yes, his number was found on Jessica Owens' phone as one of the last couple of calls she'd made, and he explained that he'd been working with her to uncover evidence of witches." Derek paused there and gave a small chuckle. "Crazy, right?"

"Oh, sure," I said, and repressed a chuckle of my own. "But what does that have to do with killing Eunice Bartlett?"

"It sounds like Dr. Grimes and Dr. Bartlett were pursuing the same thing, only he was offering a reward and she wasn't. Dr. Grimes explained that Dr. Bartlett had had a breakthrough of some kind, one that she was sure would prove the existence of witches once and for all." Derek paused there, and I could practically see him shake his head before he continued. "Once I had that information in hand, I questioned Ms. Owens further, and she reluctantly admitted that she lured Dr. Bartlett to Salem with false promises of new evidence. Once Dr. Bartlett found out Ms. Owens didn't have anything to give her, they argued. Eunice Bartlett said she was going to go to Dr. Grimes with what she had and collect the reward, and Jessica followed her out to the parking lot and then bashed her over the head with that chunk of pyrite...although she claims it was self-defense, that Dr. Grimes tried to attack her." Another pause, and I thought I heard a sigh come through the phone's speaker. "It's a mess, but I was able to reach out to Dr. Bartlett's son, and he corroborated that his mother had made some sort of discovery, even if he didn't know for sure what it was. Anyway, we've definitely got an established motive and at least a partial confession, so the D.A. is feeling pretty good about the case. I just thought I should let you know, since Jessica's shop is close to yours."

"It all sounds absolutely crazy," I said. "So... what happens now?"

"Well, we've released Trent Abernathy," Derek replied. "As for Ms. Owens, based on the brutality of the crime and the sound physical evidence, I have a feeling she's going to stay locked up until the trial. And I think we're all glad about that."

I definitely agreed with that statement—and thanked Derek for calling. He'd cleared up a few things, and I thought I could fill in the blanks on the rest. Jessica had panicked and gone to Sally for help, and while she was over at her sister's house, had probably dropped the piece of pyrite that Edgar had added to his stash. No doubt she'd been so frantic that she hadn't even realized it was missing from the much bigger chunk that had been the true murder weapon.

As for why Malcolm had asked me out, I still didn't have any real idea. Maybe, he'd been interested at first, only to realize we didn't have any true chemistry. Or maybe he'd invited me to the dance more as a way to deflect Jessica's unwanted attentions than because he was truly attracted to me, and once the date was over, he didn't have any reason to have future contact with me.

Well, besides getting the costume back so he could return it to his college's wardrobe department. I kind of doubted he'd anticipated an attack by Sally's raven while he was doing so, however. Clearly, he must have been to her house at least once, most likely in Jessica's company, even if nothing had been proven yet and no money had changed hands.

Or maybe it had. Brand-new Subarus didn't appear out of thin air, even if its owner happened to be a witch.

The important thing, though, was that my coven's spell had certainly worked the way it should.

And I'd also heard from Ruth McCoy of the Middleton coven, who'd told me that Sally had tearfully confessed everything to them.

"We're going to be keeping an eye on her," Ruth told me. "But honestly, with her sister locked up, I don't think she's going to give us any other trouble. She knows the next thing we'll do is block what little magic she has, and she wants to avoid that at all costs."

I could understand that...especially since my coven had done that very same thing to Tonya Willis after she'd been involved in all kinds of murder and mayhem. Tonya couldn't even remember that she'd once been a witch, and now lived an entirely mundane existence.

Most likely, Sally Hawkins was telling herself that even a small bit of magic was better than none at all. Maybe she deserved more of a punishment than what she was getting, but she'd have to spend the rest of her days under a cloud of suspicion, always a bit separate from the rest of her coven, and in my opinion, that was a punishment all its own.

Tuesday morning, Sage came in, all abuzz with the news. She hadn't attended the coven meeting where we'd cast the spell to trap Jessica Owens, as she'd been down in Boston with Cade Bartlett at the time.

"I can't believe Jessica is a murderer," she said. "And related to a witch!"

"Yes, it's kind of a wild situation," I replied. "I'm just glad that everything got straightened out in the end. How is Cade?"

Sage's mouth twitched just a little, telling me she'd recognized the red herring for what it was. "He's doing okay. I think it helped a lot to know that the police have his mother's killer in custody. The funeral's set for Thursday...I was kind of hoping I could have the day off to go be with him."

Even if I hadn't known it would be quiet this week, with Halloween come and gone, I still would have made the same reply.

"Of course you can take the day off. He needs his friends with him." I paused there, then figured I might as well ask. "Do you know anything about this 'breakthrough' Eunice Bartlett mentioned?"

At once, Sage's expression sobered. "Yes, she'd left a note for Cade about it, almost as though she somehow knew it might cause a problem. What she'd found was a diary from the seventeenth century, one with all sorts of descriptions of witch activity." She paused there, forest-green eyes downcast. "I saw it, Charity. It wasn't real—I mean, it's really that old, and the person who wrote it really existed. But the rest of it was made up. Our secret is still safe."

Thank God for that—I hadn't been looking forward to staging a commando raid on Eunice Bartlett's house to try to retrieve the problematic evidence.

But I only murmured, "That's good," and turned the conversation to other matters. Even so, I couldn't stop thinking about how much time Sage was spending with Cade...and how I knew deep in my gut that it probably wouldn't be too long before she came to me and said she wanted to move to Boston to be with him.

It was all right. I was happy, and I wanted her to be happy, too. The world changed, and we had to change right along with it.

That night, Noah brought some Thai takeout to my place, and we sat at the candlelit dining room table as we drank wine and shared choice morsels with the dogs, who were stationed nearby to get their share of the goodies. As dinner was winding down, though, he said, sounding almost diffident, "The lease on my house is up at the end of the month."

I set down my wine glass. "It is?" I asked, a little surprised. "I thought you moved to Salem in the spring."

Noah also put his glass on the table. "I did," he replied. "But I went to a six-month lease after my first lease ended, since I wasn't sure whether I wanted to keep renting or whether it was time to buy a house. So...."

It wasn't too hard to see where he was going with this.

Luckily, the answer was equally easy.

"So let the lease lapse and move in here," I said, and he blinked.

"Just like that?"

"Just like that," I repeated. "Or...are you not ready to take that step?"

"I'm completely ready," he said, reaching out to take my hand. "I just wanted to make sure that you were ready, too."

"It's not a very big house," I warned him, and he only chuckled.

"I think it's fine. Besides, you told me it's been added on to over the years. It's not like you don't have plenty of land for us to expand on if we decide we need a little more room."

That was true. I wouldn't want to uproot my gardens, but on the western side of the house, there was quite a bit of yard that I'd never done much with and which would give us plenty of space to grow.

"Sounds good," I said. "So give me a kiss and we'll seal the deal."

He leaned in to press his lips against mine, and in that moment, I thought of everything that lay ahead for us—Noah in this house with me and the dogs. Maybe one day, we'd have a daughter who inherited the Hughes magic, and she'd be able to grow up with both a mother and a father to raise her, the kind of family I'd never had.

Yes, I thought we would all be happy, here in our house by the sea.

This concludes the Familiar Spirits series. For more books by Christine Pope, just turn the page!

Also by Christine Pope

THE WITCHES OF MINGUS MOUNTAIN

(Paranormal Romance)

Stolen Time

Borrowed Time (January 2025)

Killing Time (February 2025)

PROJECT DEMON HUNTERS

(Paranormal Romance)

Unquiet Souls

Unbound Spirits

Unholy Ground

Unseen Voices

Unmarked Graves

Unbroken Vows

Unholy Night

THE DJINN WARS

(Paranormal Romance)

Chosen

Taken

Fallen

Broken

Forsaken

Forbidden

Awoken

Illuminated

Stolen

Forgotten

Driven

Unspoken

Hidden

Written

Given

Mistaken

FAMILIAR SPIRITS

(Cozy Mystery/Paranormal Romance)

Spells and Spaniels

Cauldrons and Cats

Hexes and Hedgehogs

Charms and Chihuahuas

Runes and Ravens

LATTES AND LEVITATION*

(Cozy Mystery/Paranormal Romance)

Caffeine Before Curses

Muffins After Magic

Pastries and Prophecies

Eclairs and Ectoplasm

Sugar Skulls and Specters

Wedding Cakes and Wishes

HEDGEWITCH FOR HIRE*

(Cozy Mystery/Paranormal Romance)

Grave Mistake

Social Medium

Household Demons

Perpetual Potion

Jingle Spells

Wandering Monsters

Uninvited Ghosts

Prophet Motive

Ballroom Bits

Spell Check

Brew Confessions

Charm School (July 2024)

UNEXPECTED MAGIC*

(Urban Fantasy/Paranormal Romance)

Found Objects

Finders, Keepers

Lost and Found

Finding Destiny

THE WITCHES OF WHEELER PARK*

(Paranormal Romance)

Storm Born

Thunder Road

Winds of Change

Mind Games

A Wheeler Park Christmas

Blood Ties

Healing Hands

Wishful Thinking

Smoke and Mirrors

MISS PRIMM'S ACADEMY FOR WAYWARD
WITCHES*

(Fantasy/Academy Romance)

Misspelled

Dispelled

Expelled

THE DEVIL YOU KNOW*

(Paranormal Romance)

Sympathy for the Devil

Charmed, I'm Sure

A Wing and a Prayer

Wish Upon a Star

THE WITCHES OF CANYON ROAD*

(Paranormal Romance)

Hidden Gifts

Darker Paths

Mysterious Ways

A Canyon Road Christmas

Demon Born

An Ill Wind

Higher Ground

Haunted Hearts

THE WITCHES OF CLEOPATRA HILL*

(Paranormal Romance)

Darkangel

Darknight

Darkmoon

Sympathetic Magic

Protector

Spellbound

A Cleopatra Hill Christmas

Impractical Magic

Strange Magic

The Arrangement

Defender

Bad Blood

Deep Magic

Darktide

THE WATCHERS TRILOGY*

(Paranormal Romance)

Falling Dark

Dead of Night

Rising Dawn

THE SEDONA FILES*

(Paranormal/Science Fiction Romance)

Bad Vibrations

Desert Hearts

Angel Fire

Star Crossed

Falling Angels

Enemy Mine

TALES OF THE LATTER KINGDOMS*

(Fantasy Romance)

All Fall Down

Dragon Rose

Binding Spell

Ashes of Roses

One Thousand Nights

Threads of Gold

The Wolf of Harrow Hall

Moon Dance

The Song of the Thrush

THE GAIAN CONSORTIUM SERIES*

(Science Fiction Romance)

Beast (free prequel novella)

Blood Will Tell

Breath of Life

The Gaia Gambit

The Mandala Maneuver

The Titan Trap

The Zhore Deception

The Refugee Ruse

STANDALONE TITLES

Hearts on Fire (Paranormal Romance)

Taking Dictation (Contemporary Romance)

Golden Heart (Gaslamp Fantasy Romance)

Night Music: A Modern Reimagining of The Phantom
of the Opera (Contemporary Romance)

Ghost Dance: A Sequel to Gaston Leroux's The
Phantom of the Opera (Historical Mystery/Romance)

Flight Before Christmas (Fantasy Romance)

* Indicates a completed series

About the Author

USA Today bestselling author Christine Pope has been writing stories ever since she commandeered her family's Smith-Corona typewriter back in grade school. Her work includes paranormal romance, cozy paranormal mystery, and urban fantasy, among others. She makes her home in Arizona.

Christine Pope on the Web:
www.christinepope.com

f facebook.com/ChristinePopeAuthor
P pinterest.com/ChristineJPope
BB bookbub.com/authors/christine-pope